The Watchman of Salt and Dust

Svyatoslav Bratva Romance

by Rada Lyubomirova

***

Neurodivergent Version

***

Alpha Eureka Edukasia, Inc., 2023.

First published on October 31st '2023.

Cover Photo by Andrew Poplavsky

Digital Version ISBN: **978-1-963038-69-9**

Paperback Print ISBN: **979-8-9884575-5-8**

Hardcover Print ISBN: **978-1-963038-56-9**

Travel Version ISBN: **978-1-963038-32-3**

Neurodivergent ISBN: **978-1-963038-13-2**

***

Alpha Eureka Edukasia, Inc., DE, USA.

https://www.compendiapublishing.com

FAIR WARNING

This publication contains explicit language, explicit romantic scenes, uncommon courtship, and depictions of the forced mobilisation of men and women. Readers' discretion is advised.

This work of fiction is NOT suitable for minors. The age limits may vary from one area of jurisdiction to another. In the absence of clear guidance and/or limitations from the governing bodies, the publisher and the author suggest that 21 years of age be the minimum age for reading this publication.

DISCLAIMER

This book is a work of fiction that draws inspiration from a Southeast Asian folktale, the duties of the Patron Saints, and historical events in Eastern Europe.

This work of fiction is for entertainment purposes only and is NOT to be treated as a matter of fact or as the ground for theories. Some parts are added for dramatic purposes. However, this publication may be treated as a subject to study in the language arts, literature, culture, psychology, or any other related department or faculty.

The manuscript and cover of this literary work are not generated by artificial intelligence and may NOT be utilised for AI training without the written permission of the copyright owner.

The background story in the last part of this book provides a list of the names of the characters in this book. Eastern European households have different naming systems that might be confusing for some.

All forms of names and their functions are explained for the readers to easily read this story.

Also by Rada Lyubomirova

To understand who the Great One and his wife are,
kindly read the **"LILITH AND SAMAEL"** book series.
Book 1—A Story of the Twin Flame
Book 2—The House of Alchemists
Book 3—The Guardian Prince of Rome

***

SLAVA DEITY
Lord of the Underworld: A Paranormal Shifter
Romance of Veles
Springtime Birth and Wintertime Rebirth:
A Psychic Paranormal Romance of Yarilo and Morana

Dedication

To the patron who shelters the good girl in his arms, that's more than enough—much stronger pillars than bricks and stones.

To the good girl who has been away from her origin, remember that home is here and now; seek refuge under the warmth of the patron's arms.

Prologue
Kolya

Around A Decade Ago

***

He handed me a letter, which I assumed was from his past life. A life that he needed to burn in the fire he was igniting.

Those arks and metal birds are tools for the dust to be in command of.

The sky, the constellations, and the wind speak to us, deck crews.

Especially when it is time for us to make life-or-death split-second decisions.

They are the handiwork of the Guardian.

They are for us to seek Guidance.

Not for the dust to control them.

When the handiworks are on the move, they are for the dust to watch and listen to.

Once one little flower falls, she will not be among the dust.

The little flower will become the sky flower to fly higher.

She will be surrounding you.

Within the air you breathe in, moving the oxygen in the blood for you to keep going forward.

Within the atmosphere, armouring your flesh with protection.

Within the wind, whispering Guidance whenever you are in command of the artillery.

Within the whispers, the wisdom will be relayed.

"Who is she?"

"The flower in the higher sky." He took out a name patch. Sánchez was embroidered on it. "And whose is that?"

"The name belonged to a Saint."

"You haven't mentioned your name, soldier."

"Saint."

"The Saints only passed, but didn't die."

"But this one has."

RADA LYUBOMIROVA

***

With the permission of the author, this prologue
was taken from the book:

1

Bunking In

Kolya

They had become filthier by trafficking the younger ones. The more days passed by, the younger the catch. The ones we caught yesterday shouldn't be on their ship; those women should be staying at school, even learning at university. Probably only three to five of the women had passed the age to make their own decisions, but the rest of them hadn't quite yet.

The movement became more unpredictable. There used to be schedules for cargo deliveries, but lately, those traffickers went rogue. There were fewer girls and women left to traffic from the origin. With much less money they could possibly make from fewer commodities, they became more reckless. As much as it was bitter in my tongue to refer to them as 'commodities,' that was how the traffickers saw those women.

I knew myself enough to want a slut of my own. My future wife would be my personal sex slave to toy with. The right one would beg me to use her like a property I own.

There was some advantage to being the youngest one; I got the chance to watch and learn from my brothers. They had their own way of treating their women. Of course, they were different from one another. They had their own partners to fuck, but Adya was the first to be married. He was the only one married.

Natasha, his wife, was always nurturing when building a home for him. But at other times, she knew how to, let's say, slap him in the head, proving him wrong by having bigger balls than him.

Adya called her Tashenka, or *Zhizn' Moya*, which meant my life. He has had a different kind of life since marrying her. When they were still dating, there was a time when he opened their relationship. Natasha got her first side-dick only hours after he opened it. He went for months without any of his crushes being fruitful in his bed. I found him hilarious to watch, though. She gave him her list of body counts during their open relationship. By the time he closed their relationship again, he fucked zero side-pussy.

Despite the fact that Adya overvalued himself, he now understood that she was way above market value. He should have been grateful for the smart and beautiful partner he had. It was a relief for us that Adya decided to marry her.

In their marriage, Natasha agreed to his free-use terms. He took her whenever his dick became hard or wherever there was a place. This hall was one of the times and places. He ate her pussy on the same table where we were eating our supper. He didn't care about others seeing her naked. As long as his dick, or fingers, or even tongue were in one of her holes, he looked proud to show off his wife.

The way he praised her in front of everybody else was something I learnt so much from. He told her precisely what to do and how to do it at what moment. Natasha wasn't shy about obeying her husband in front of the audience.

When he told her to come, she came for him. And only for him, because in her mind we disappeared. Compliments after compliments that he gave her were only to make her care less about anything or anyone around her. She did nothing but follow her husband's command.

That was how he dominated her, by giving her pleasure. He got satisfaction by satisfying her. It might sound like a long rerouting, but it made sense to me. Although he let everyone watch, Adya wouldn't share his wife with anyone.

Others watched them with their own partners. When they couldn't watch any longer, my other brothers or their partners started their own show. I used to be one of them watching, but not since I left Lyena.

No one would mind me continuing my supper tonight; I even ate more than I should have eaten. My cock sometimes rebelled against my brain.

After I finished, I walked to the other room, where there were beds to bunk in. When I opened the door, the women inside were immediately on guard. They were getting close to one another, covering their bodies with anything they could reach.

2

Slipping Away

Kolya

Here we were, the five of us. The rain hadn't stopped for two days; none of us had any proper food to eat since then. We needed to find our other two brothers and another one who was like a brother to us.

"Do you want to go to the river or not? We gotta eat, Kolya. We can't see which plant to eat."

"Yeah, I know, Hristo. River's in the opposite direction from the three. The clue leads to the waterfall."

Adya came with two spears made of the thickest branches we could find. "There. The so-called spears should be enough to get us some fish in the river."

"That is, if we go to the river," Hristo said.

"What do you mean? I thought we agreed to find food before finding the others."

Hristo shrugged his shoulders, then signalled that it was me who had a different idea.

"Let me go up first." I started climbing the tree to see better. The pouring rain kept me slipping down again and again. I was only nine at the time, almost ten. With not much left that I had in me without any food, it got harder to climb up after each slip.

"Sir." I heard a woman's voice and a small hand shaking my shoulder. "Sir, please. You're terrifying the younger ones."

My gun was out and pointed at them. When I finally woke up from my sleep, I saw either terror or rage in those eyes. Compassion had left their feminine eyes a long time ago. I'd prefer to see rage in those women's eyes. It could be practical for the project.

"You three, come with me," I said to them with rage in their eyes. I led them out of the room towards the hall.

When they saw some of my brothers still in their underpants from the previous orgy, those women grabbed anything close to their hands to use as weapons. Their raging eyes were wide open.

"Butter knives or boots aren't lethal enough to murder any of us. Besides, our balls are already emptied. Well, except Kolya. Good luck with emptying those of his." Adya always enjoyed his time making fun of me. It was his way of saying that

I needed to move on with my life. I loved my brother still, but I'd better not make his ego bigger by saying that he was right.

Walking towards the sink to wash my face, I kept reminding myself that my princess was gone. Leaving her was the best decision for the both of us. I couldn't save anyone unless they wanted to save themselves first from drowning in their dark world. Even if they wanted to be pulled out of drowning, I could only help so much to transport them to safe ground. What happened after that was their decision to make, not mine.

My bedsheets had been too tidy for a while now. So I'd prefer to sleep somewhere else rather than in my own bed. It was easier that way to hijack my brain.

None of them were putting away their cute weapons. "What do you want from us?"

"Since you have nothing to offer, I don't think that's the right question here. Fuck, you couldn't even let me sleep."

"If that twitching was called sleeping, you should be grateful I woke you up. Besides, your mumbling horror terrified the younger ones."

"Can we throw this one back into the ocean? Sharks might be hungry by now," I said while looking towards Hristo.

"Please, have a seat. Or not, it's up to you. You can call me Hristo. I'm older than the other boys, but we follow the youngest one. That one, you can call him Kolya."

"Why would you follow the youngest one? How old is he anyway?"

"Old enough for Daddying you in bed. You passed eighteen, yeah?"

"Twenty, actually." From her looks alone, I could have Daddied her in bed. With the rage in her eyes, the ten years gap between us might not mean anything. With proper training, she could be a more lethal shadow-worker than me one day.

"Look, I only need to know where you're taking us. We were already trafficked. So if you don't help us, you'd better kill us early on. All of us would consider it a mercy."

"Huh? You agree, then, to feeding the sharks? Marvellous. Quick in and out project. Can I go to sleep now?"

"Oh my days, this baby. Off you go now. Bed. Or sofa, whichever you choose."

"Got it. I sleep, and you play with the shark food." I crashed my body onto the sofa where they fucked earlier. It still smelt like sex. I tried so much to close my eyes and catch some sleep before transporting tomorrow.

This project was unexpected. We were supposed to be on Slava for another family occasion, but a suspicious ship intercepted our course. Then we jumped into the submarine to fish out those women around Zembra.

This base in Palermo was the closest shelter. It was rather ancient, but necessary in a time like this. It was important for us to get to a shelter as soon as possible. We then assessed if the cargo was truly cargo or simply a diversion.

Hristo's voice was still loud in my ears, explaining our plan. Briefly, he talked about getting out of Italy and the different routes to Switzerland. He knew the rules, so he didn't talk about anything unnecessary. The volume of his voice became lower in my ears. My eyelids were heavier. Then my mind slipped into the realm of the underworld.

3

Shifters

Kolya

9 years old

The monkeys ate it. If they ate it and were still breathing after that, we could be eating them, too. I slipped down from the tree easily because of the rain. Once my feet touched the wet ground, I walked in the direction of the fruit plant.

Kolman stopped me. "Ey, waterfall that way, river this way."

"Follow my footsteps."

"I know better where to go with rafts, but I'm with Kolman on this."

"There. Listen to Mobhi if you don't want to listen to me."

"You've heard me. Follow my footsteps."

They followed me anyway. I wasn't sure if they followed me as their leader. Surely they followed me so they wouldn't lose me. Otherwise, mother would be fuming, and they'd be in trouble with their fathers.

While walking in a different direction than we were supposed to, I looked up once in a while. The trees truly looked similar from below. Finally, I stopped under the fruit tree that the monkey ate. "Anyone wants to climb and get our food? You know, take turns climbing."

"Next time, you tell us *why* we're going somewhere. If you want to make things work, learn how to talk. Use your words, Kolyasha. We can't read your brain," Mobhi said.

"If I were speaking what my brain told me, would you not argue with me? Father said that we cannot buy time. Why waste it by fighting?"

After eating that day, we followed Kolman and Mobhi. We brought some of the fruits for the other three. The clues and tracks led us to the waterfall. That night, we stopped to take some rest in a cave.

"Kolyasha, talk," Hristo said.

"What's to talk about?"

"I don't know. What's in your brain, maybe?"

"Of course, you start with that," Adya added. Kolman and Mobhi joined the circle beside him.

"Aren't we supposed to sleep, yes?"

"Huh, let's pretend that your brain ever slept. I agree with Adya." Hristo was always the big guy, not only in his body but also in his character. He knew how to invite me to speak if I was thinking about something but didn't have the clue to deliver it in words.

"The sky and wind talk to Mobhi and Kolman more than to me. You know where we are and where to go." I paused, looking at my two brothers in turn. "So I know I won't be lost if I'm you."

"Where did this come from again?"

"It's just always there inside of my brain, Adya. You're good at making things to hunt. Joe looks at the things you made. If he sees they're safe, he gives them to me. Klima and Seva are like Joe. Actually, the three of them worry about me a lot."

"And what about you?"

"I have nothing to worry about, Hristo. You know, I'm okay being the baby. I like watching you slap their heads when they're fighting."

We continued our track in the morning to the waterfall. Neither Seva, Klima, nor Joe were around the waterfall. We found cordages of roots hanging from the tree beside it. The three of them apparently climbed down from where they were. Not far away from it, we heard their voices bantering with each other. "We thought you were never coming. We almost finished all the fish we trapped," Joe said.

"We made a detour. The baby wanted to get some fruit first. Here, he got you some."

Klima's unfinished raft was slightly wonky and unbalanced. With more hands, we could ready the raft to set sail. It took the rest of the day for us to finish it, so we decided to sail the next morning.

We trusted Mobhi to plan for the journey back to our parents. Along the way, our mentors watched us sail the river. They sat there under the tree by the riverside. We bowed to the fiery eyes of the tigers.

After the roots in the front were done, I turned around to continue making cordage for the end tail. None of my brothers turned around after we passed the seven.

All seven turned into walking on two feet. I watched them walk towards the river. All their hands were clasping in front of their human bodies. They bowed to me, smiling warmly.

I looked around to watch my brothers and Joe. None of them were aware of our mentors shifting. When I turned my head back again, none of the seven were there.

***

Kolya

Vibrating.

"Kolyasha? Joe."

"Speak."

"Hey, I just want to catch up before we officiate."

"Ah, yes, it's today. We felt bad about suddenly leaving. It's important for you, and you're one of us."

"That's what I wanted to talk about. Hold on, I'll put you on speaker."

"Hey, Kolya. We have Lance here. Mia is in her suite," said Sandy. "Well, we can't be seeing her, can we?"

"Sandy, Lance. I'm sorry that we won't be attending your weddings today. Can we pay it off at the celebration?"

"We discussed this with Mia over the phone last night. We can actually—"

"We have plenty of time to celebrate later on when we board the mothership."

"What happened with the 'We cannot buy time' stuff you always said again?"

"That's my point. It's something important to you. So you shouldn't be wasting time only to include us. Joe, you're one of us, and you'll always be. But we aren't more important than the family that you're about to build."

"Yeah, but I wouldn't even have survived in the past if it weren't for you, fam. And the mentors, too."

"Well, I'd like to say, 'Wedding is only a beginning, not merely the end,' but my last relationship didn't make it to the wedding day."

"Ooh, you better bring the potential backpack to our celebration. That is, if there is any."

"I'll tell our brothers that you called because you got nervous. You get cold feet; we break your neck. You hurt her if she's right; we slit your throat."

"Oh, I gave up debating you a long time ago."

"No, I'm talking to all three of you."

Lance answered, "I've never known you Svyatoslavs personally, but... a covenant it is with the Bratva."

"A covenant it is with the House of Zhou," I said to Lance.

"So is that a yes or no about the potential backpack?"

"I can't recall when you're asking a question. Need to go, Joe. Transport day."

"Unbelievable—" I cut him off.

My sleep sometimes brought me back to a reminiscence about the past. I stayed on the sofa for a while. It was a good time back then. Until it wasn't.

4

Her Watchman

Kolya

"You've been staring at it for a while. If you come in, I'm sure that Cathedral will still be here when you come out of it."

"Oh, I'm not a follower. I just admire the design. It's gothic."

"Neither am I a follower of their rites. Would you like to come inside? It wouldn't be so strange when two visitors admire it together."

"Then we'd be lost together inside, and no one would notice? I like that idea."

"Shall we?" I followed her. At the entrance of St. Nicholas Cathedral, she paused without saying anything.

"You make a cross. Like this." I showed her how to make a cross with the holy water, the Latin rite's one. I paid attention to her when she mimicked what I did.

Her anxiety was showing, as if she were making a mistake, and she didn't want anyone to know. She gazed at how majestic the Cathedral was. Her body was already considerably smaller than mine, and inside of here, she actually appeared adorably small.

I followed where her curiosity led, as she became my personal walking curiosity. Her curiosity about the Cathedral and my curiosity about her all collided.

Her reflective eyes enchanted me. I wondered how the hazel would look when they turned greenish in the autumn. Her long, curled eyelashes swept me away when she blinked. Her stern, arched eyebrows held me in place. I wondered if my place should be inside of her.

"You don't need to stay with me if you need to be somewhere else."

"This is where I need to be. Following you is better than being suspected as an intruder, or worse, a spy."

She chuckled. "Are you a spy?"

"I could be one if you want me to."

"I've never met a spy or an intruder before. I'm curious about how they work. I mean, do they watch someone from afar? Or barge into someone's house undetected? Technically, Father Christmas intrudes on everyone's houses to leave those gifts."

"Technically speaking, not everyone's house. I couldn't agree more with him, though; a good girl deserves her reward. Be careful of what you wish for, because someone might come to deliver."

"I'm not sure you want to dye your dusty blond hair white like snow."

"Neither am I, firehead."

***

Kolya
Six Months Later

That day, when I met her for the first time, the firehead ignited the flame inside me. It wasn't a small fire that she ignited. It was a burn-to-ashes kind of flame.

People said that eyes were the window of the soul, but not hers. Those hazel eyes reflected her surroundings, including me when I was near her. They gave me the reflection that I needed, just like I was looking at myself in the mirror. I didn't like to stare at my reflection. But through her eyes, I was almost wishing to get lost in her realm.

She should have been careful with what she wished for. That was precisely what I had been doing to my good girl—showering her with rewards that she deserved. Even if she wasn't being a good girl one day, she'd better know how to earn it.

Nothing tangible seemed to be important to her. Not in an ungrateful way, but in a way that she appreciated kindness, values, people, connections, processes, and even life itself. She didn't collect things. She collected knowledge, experience, and even memories.

She liked being in the library until late. If the library wasn't closing, I bet she would have continued burying herself in books tonight. She worked hard for the midterm. Actually, she had been working hard all the time.

"Let me read her work later, when she's asleep."

Her having to walk alone at this late hour of the night was never something that I liked. She was lucky that I had sniper skills. I could watch her walk home at night like this.

To warn the man approaching her from the dark corner, I sent a bullet to the bottle in his hand. Alma caught the sound of the breaking glass. She then became aware of him. Then she walked a bit faster than before.

"Run faster, little spark! The next one I'm firing is to his head."

Once she was inside her place, I left the roof. I needed to buy some things she might need. She hadn't gotten supplies for the winter yet. If she were with me, she wouldn't have to worry about basic needs. I wouldn't let her worry about anything.

Although I'd love to have her in my life, it wouldn't be fair if I asked her to leave everything behind. Surely, anyone who knew how she worked would offer her a job. But I wouldn't ask her to choose between me and her study. I knew how hard she worked for it because it was something important to her. So I enjoyed my time watching her from afar. I was still figuring out how to provide for her from far away. Providing for her was something important to me.

Hidden cameras were already planted inside her place. They were for me to watch over her. It was for her safety and my own pleasure. The most pleasurable time for me was the morning after I left gifts under my good girl's pillow.

Whenever she found those, she held her reward close to her chest. The gifts stayed on her chest. But her soft hands moved down to her delicious-looking breasts. As if even the remains of my presence could get her off that easily, one of hers moved further down to play with her pussy.

She held me in her mind when the wave of her pleasure came. That pleasure was the true reward that my good girl deserved. Only by watching did she drown my cock in my own pleasure. If only it were inside of her and not in my own fist.

I knew that she was aware of me watching her. I couldn't help it; she was amusing to watch. My puzzle to solve. My curiosity to follow. My precious thing to guard. She was mine to keep.

The maskman might be easy for anyone to fall for, especially those with particular kinks. They thought it was about the layers of fabric that the mask had. They had no clue that it was actually about layers of shadow that lay between the layers of flesh behind the mask. I wasn't sure if the face behind this mask was ever worthy of her.

5

Rooting

Alma

When walking under the full moon like this, the chill always made the hair at the back of my neck rise. I wasn't the one scared of werewolves or vampires, but more of humans with bad intentions. I wanted to leave earlier, but I couldn't, not before finishing my paper for the midterm.

The wind sent the scent of fear and terror to some, but for me, it was the scent of security. It told me that I was safe to walk alone at this hour of the night. The wind breezed the scent of *him*. It had been about six months since the first time I was aware of such a scent. Up until the middle of my second semester, I never realised that such a scent even existed in this world. It wasn't simply his perfume that I sensed. Something else that belonged only to him told me that he was close.

My first year away from Berlin was rather challenging. I left the one place I knew for good. Pursuing my master's degree on full scholarship was enough reason to leave my family behind. It was also the most logical reason that they wouldn't drag me away from leaving.

Other than studying, I worked four hours on Friday and two full days on the weekend to feed myself. The chef sometimes gave me leftovers from his kitchen. Usually, it was enough for me to split it into two—one half for supper and the other half for breakfast the next day.

The owner of the restaurant was generous enough to give me a job. Not to mention, let me rent a space above it. A much cheaper place than any other in the city of Fribourg. My space was more than enough for me alone. The owner gave me a vacant space with a bed, a shower, and a kitchenette.

Thankfully, I didn't have to pass everyone to enter; the door to my place was a different entrance from the restaurant. I locked the door behind me, pretending that it would do anything different to prevent my maskman from entering. He wasn't lost when he entered because the stairs led only to my place.

I managed to buy a carpet from the serving tips, which was enough for me to study and eat on the floor in front of the old fireplace. It wasn't common for anyone to give a tip to servers here, but I appreciate those who did. Taking a shower helped me sleep in the night like this. Washing my hair and using a conditioner were good enough pampering for me. I hadn't earned enough money to even think about luxury.

"Good night, guard. Thank you for watching over me and guarding me home," I said to him before resting my eyes, although I wasn't sure where the word 'home' took place.

Everytime I smelt his scent, I always woke up to find gifts the next morning. He put them under my pillow. Or beside it, if he gave me some flowers.

He gave me sweets, small bites, and even some daily things that I didn't know I might need. I loved it when he slid some chocolate when I had my period. I couldn't afford it, but somehow he knew. Sometimes I wondered if there was any surveillance camera he planted at my place. He gave me things I needed at specific times that I had never told anyone. He was always thoughtful with me.

When I woke up this morning, there was something my hand felt under the pillow. My eyes weren't fully awake yet, but I tried to reach for my gift. A half of me always hoped that my maskman was there. *He* should be my gift, but he wasn't this morning—another disappointment.

This time, I found sticky notes, with a note on the first one that said, *"Read carefully, little spark. Then write them down."* He wrote the note in cursive, so he must be older than me. People my age or younger might not write in cursive anymore, although I could still read them.

I closed my eyes again, inhaling his remaining scent. My twenty-six-year-old self suddenly turned back into a teenager after receiving a letter from her crush. I held his note with both hands and placed it on my chest. His aura touched my neck while I was imagining him giving me a necklace. I could almost feel the fingers from his other hand playing with my hardened nipples. As I played with my breasts, I pretended that his mouth was devouring them.

When he was satisfied making my breasts his toy, I imagined that he would trace down my abdomen. When I finally woke up to him one day, I would serve my pussy as his breakfast. Only the thought of his warm tongue made me produce more juice for him.

My maskman was always sweet by sending me gifts, but deep down, I never wanted him to be sweet when he took me. I wished he would make me his own gift toy to play with. Becoming his living sex doll would fulfil my purpose—to let myself be under his patronage. All these times, he put me under his care. So I should be put in my place when he finally takes me.

"Would he be mad if I came without his permission?"

Just like right now, I came to my hand without his permission. If there were indeed surveillance cameras, I wanted him to watch me. He needed to know how much I craved his touch. His arms must have felt like home when I recovered from my orgasm and snuggled in them.

While opening my eyes, I came back from his realm. The morning ray of light peaked through the curtain. It was enough to brighten my place. I rolled over on my bed, only to find every page of my paper hung on the wall. Not a single page was unharmed. He left notes all over them, in cursive Cyrrilic.

"How many languages does my maskman speak?"

Even though I chose a master's in Slavic studies, I took minor studies in history. Not because I needed to, but only to prolong my time in this city. I was secretly hoping to meet him in person without his mask on.

I was writing about ancient Slavic history for my midterm paper. Or I thought I was, considering those red notes he put on almost every paragraph. My paper became scraps in his hands. He might be one of the lecturers at the uni. He surprised me with how much knowledge he had on the subject.

Actually, he surprised me each time I smelt his scent around.

When reading the notes he left, I couldn't believe that I obviously missed so many details on my paper. I tried to focus on the base and the root of the ancient Slavic, but apparently it wasn't rooted enough.

He wasn't only focussing on the details of my draft but also the placement. There were circles and arrows to note which section should be written in which order. He might be working as a structural book editor. Or he might be one of the lecturers at the uni who edited manuscripts for publications. Regardless, he was right; I needed to make revisions to it. Using the sticky notes, I wrote down things that I needed to research further in the library.

Through the corner of my eyes, I realised that he left me some bread in my kitchenette. There was another sticky note on the refrigerator door saying, "It's stocked, *in case my little spark hasn't gone shopping. No skipping meals when I'm not around!*"

He knew. Last winter was so hard on everyone that the restaurant didn't make that much from the serving fee to share with every staff member. He somehow knew that I sometimes skipped meals to prepare for the upcoming winter. There were eggs, milk, butter, meat, and other things inside. My cupboard was full of supplies.

He called me *his* little spark. In the most uncommon way, he took care of me. It felt weird not knowing to whom I should send my gratitude. While making breakfast from what he gave me, I realised how much I didn't know about him or even where to find him. After showering, I put all the drafts and notes inside of my bag before leaving my place.

6

Upgrades

Kolya

The people in the north would need us on the ground during the autumn and especially in the winter. The Great One used to guard the North of his origin. He passed the legacy to us, the Svyatoslavs, to guard the north of the earth, along with what they used to call Thrace. The institution assigned me to watch over Russia, particularly Moskwa, and Greece in general. Parts of Switzerland, especially Fribourg, were an addition to it.

As for the sea, we watched over those seafarers, especially the shadow-workers on the mothership, Slava. We could only do projects in the sea and on the road during the spring and summer. Every sea project needed to be done before the beginning of autumn. The seven of us were summoned to Berlin after finishing our last sea project.

"Is there any particular reason for these upgrades?"

"It became too old for you. You've become messier on projects," Gunther said.

"Oh, come on. Two years is considered old, you said? I love the shit."

"It wasn't the bike. We've told him too many times to get his dick wet. He just didn't listen," said Adya.

"Since when my dick became your concern?"

The Great One entered the motor plant. "These younglings couldn't be left on their own."

"As always, my Great One." I gave him a bow. "I couldn't see the urgency to upgrade our bikes at the moment."

"You need to watch while overcoming terrain." He actually made sense about the dual-sport bike to watch from the higher ground. But I could tell that the 1300 cc was much heavier than my old 1000 cc sports bike. Readjusting from a four-cylinder in-line engine to a twin-cylinder boxer engine would be needed.

"But I agree that you've become messier lately."

"I'm not sure I follow."

"Russia, Greece, and Switzerland were given to you to watch over. You indeed need to preserve Fribourg. We need to maintain neutral ground to be neutral. It was never meant to neglect the vast to pay attention to one little, tiny one. You weren't having favourites, were you?"

"It depends on which favourite we are to have."

"Nonetheless, the so-called potential backpack needs to be turned in," Milady said while entering the plant. She let the shiny hair down most of the time, but today she wore her beautiful black hair in a braid. She was intimidating to many, but somehow she let her husband Daddying her. "It isn't always easy to partner with any shadow-worker. With you being a Watchman, you're to lead others working on projects."

"Milady," I said without any other words.

"My love, imagine how she'd react to seeing our libraries." His face turned from his wife towards me. The Great One obviously implied some points about Alma. "Oh, Nika, there are reasons why we've been called the Watchers. Unlike Watchmen, we still get our wings intact."

"So, you've been watching my movement, then."

"Since when did I stop watching your movement?"

Both the Great One and I turned our faces towards my brothers. They either crossed their arms while holding their laughter, raised their hands with a giving-up gesture, or even shrugged their shoulders.

"We gave up arguing with this baby brat ("brother") a long time ago," said Adya.

"Have I ever argued with any of you?"

"That's my point. Do you know what I mean? You don't argue. You'd rather give us silence, sit there, and wait for us to make confessions. Or wait for us to face the consequences for not listening to you."

Rhetorically, I asked, "Can we move on now?"

The Great One asked, "Can you, Nika? Not from your brother, of course."

I followed their guide for our measurement. Other shadow-workers were provided with vehicles for projects, but not like us. Our vehicles of choice were measured and adjusted according to our bodies. They weren't transferable to anyone other than us, the riders.

It was Sevastyan Romanov who took care of our motorbikes. By keeping track of the maintenance, he made sure that all ours were in good condition for the project. Seva also made adjustments for other shadow-workers if they had particular projects. Practically, my brother slept in the garage.

Seva and Adya were pretty excited about their bikes. From 1000 to 1254 cc replacements, but they remained riding sports bikes. The only thing that upset them was when they were told to switch to double-breasted suits. For them, it was either double-breasted suits or they kept wearing single-breasted under the gears. I could only imagine the sweat. From what I saw, it was their negotiation skills that needed some upgrades.

Mobhi, Klima, and I remained in single-breasted suits for projects. Hristo and Kolman were all right with adding waistcoats under their single-breasted suits. They were mature enough to understand the safety measurements for their short-range combat on the road. They were to keep riding their power cruisers.

We wore suits that were chosen for us. All suits depended on each person's duty or the type of project we handled. Like others, our suits had bulletproof layers underneath. But unlike others, ours also had protectors underneath. I had no clue how the tailors combined class and safety, but they made it work somehow.

Our submarine needed more time for this upgrading plan that the Great One had in mind. Since autumn was coming in a few weeks, it was time for us to go to the motherland.

7

Fathers' Legacy

It was -30°C in Yakutsk, the capital of Yakutia. We were to expect the temperature to worsen in the winter. It was only the last day of October. Koloman Mac Feidhlimidh and Brendan Mac Finlugh referred to it as Samhain, while others might refer to it as Halloween. Our celebration would begin after sunset with a bonfire. My brothers wearing my family name never meant to completely remove their culture.

Kolman's father, Feidhlimidh, was a brother-in-suffering of Mobhi's father, Finlugh. In the middle of the night, the pirates abducted them from their villages. They had endured slavery, lashes, and chains on a daily basis. Living, sitting, and breathing only to work on that pirate ship. They were the reason we decided to do projects related to human trafficking.

After father passed away, those two Irish men immediately stepped up to fulfil the role. Both of them raised me in two polar opposite ways. It was indeed necessary to raise me in such a way.

Feidhlimidh taught me about consistency when doing a job. He was the one who taught me to endure. Even in the most uncomfortable situations, he always got the job done.

"Not only done, but done in the right manner, Nika. Only because no one is watching, it was never meant that we shouldn't do it in the right manner," Feidhlimidh said.

Finlugh, on the contrary, was always sunny and warm. He smiled a lot compared to us, the Rus. We weren't necessarily to smile on every occasion; even our banter was cold and dark. Somehow, I felt like Adya got a high sense of humour from Finlugh.

As a father figure, he taught me to see the bright side of things. He always reminded me to be grateful for each moment and cherish it in any possible way. He sang, too, when he told the tales. The way he did it was almost like a comedy show around the bonfire.

Some said those two men combined could be lethal, and lethal they were. Wherever they were, they managed to find their way out—or their way in. I felt privileged to get under those Irishmen's wings. We, the Svyatoslavs, were privileged enough to call them fathers. The story of their clans was close to being erased from existence. Their history of forced mobilisation seemed to be drowning, as if the records had been forced to walk the plank into the ocean without anyone knowing it. We were the only legacy of our Irish fathers to survive to tell the tale and sing their ballad.

Those two fathers of ours fathered two of the most reliable navigators that we could ever have. They made sure to find our way, even when we were tangled in the darkest mischief. Like fathers, like sons.

Although I wanted to have my own children, I questioned myself a lot. I wasn't sure whether I'd be a good father one day. With Lyena in the past, of course, it came to my mind now and then to start a family. But it all disappeared when she chose to return to her dark life and to enjoy finding comfort in other men's beds.

Alma hit me differently. She made me think about starting a family with her. She took care of her family well, even though it didn't end up so well before she left them. She had been working hard to make ends meet on top of studying. She stretched out her resources to make it on her own two feet. Even though she didn't have so much on her own, she always seemed grateful.

She made me want to take care of her. Little did she know that I had been paying the less fortunate people to eat at the restaurant. I told them to tip her big. It was a win-win for both parties. Those people had their meals while I kept providing for Alma, even when I wasn't close to her. Most of them were good enough people to do as I told them. A couple of those arseholes weren't. When they kept the tip for themselves, I gave them some lessons to learn. Fortunately, I had the resources, as a sniper, to watch them from afar.

When I was close to Alma, I found comfort in wearing my mask. I knew it wasn't fair that I could see her while she couldn't. That way, I took advantage of her. Only by watching her sleep did she calm me down. The way her breasts moved up and down weaved my sound mind back into my head. Those breasts looked so delicious, which always made my cock rebel against my trousers.

Listening to her breathing brought a sense of home. I recorded her inside of my head so I could recall it whenever I needed her with me. In a time like this, I needed her the most—to calm me down while I patiently waited for my target.

It had been almost four hours since I laid my stomach down on this bed of snow. For that long, my balls had been frozen. The thought of emptying my balls inside of my little spark gave me enough heat to survive this cold. If my cock was a gun, her pussy must be the holster to keep me secure.

All I could do was hold onto my rifle and keep watching through the scope. There were huge differences in operating in the north than anywhere else, especially in this weather condition. Those younger snipers tended to pick the newer rifles, but I was all right with this one.

They said that mine would cover 1,500 metres. That wasn't the case in my hand. This one could go further and beyond. Sometimes, it was more about the man behind the rifle. They were tools and equipment to complete the project, not entirely something to praise too much. Similar to motorbikes, they were vehicles, depending on the bikers, or just like the submarine, depending on the sailors, or any other type of vehicle in general. I believed aviators believed it in a similar way.

"Damn, I miss the old shit." But what can I say? The Great One said it was time to upgrade my motorbike.

Yuren finally arrived and entered the hall with his guards. He was bad, but his sister was worse. Tonight, she wasn't joining. The chief of the city centre welcomed him.

Those women and their guardians stayed in the hall. I could have taken the shot by now, as they were walking to his office. None of the women or their parents would even know what this was all about, but where was the fun in it?

They must be promised a modelling or acting job abroad. They were indeed beautiful; I wasn't blind about that. They could have used social media to go viral and earn income nowadays. Their parents or guardians might not have any clue what those women were getting into. From what I was seeing, Yuren planned to board those women on a private jet.

"Damn you, chief! Is that how much they're worth to you? At least set the number higher for the family to survive the winter."

The chief checked every bit of the money inside of the suitcase. Either his greed or stupidity clouded his judgement. It could be both.

"Take the shot, Crown. We can't get Samhain to pass," said Mobhi on the radio.

"Relax... Relax. Let me play with my food."

Yuren and the chief were leaving the office to return to the hall. They shook some of the women's hands. I no longer had a clear shot of either Yuren or the chief. I waited a little longer. Then it was out, flying—a bullet for Yuren. I sent another one for the chief.

Horror and panic filled the hall with the blood splash. I sent another bullet to the exit door, and I watched them heading for the other exit. But again, I needed to lead them in the right direction. My next one was flying towards the last way out. They followed my lead to the deceased chief's office. I sent my last bullet towards the suitcase lock. They deserved all the money, though I was still fuming about the number.

When clearing up my trace from the ground, at a glance, I saw him approaching towards me. He wasn't exactly landing; he waved-off to pick me up.

"For fuck's sake, Nika, I thought you didn't plan to pull the trigger. As your brothers said, you've been messier."

"But they can use the money to cover their needs, my Great One. The number should be higher, though. Those fuckers didn't even follow the fucking market price."

Kolman said, *"Crown, where the fuck are you? What are you planning to miss Samhain now?"*

"Up in the air—"

"Crown is needed elsewhere."

"Wings?"

"Celtic, I'll get him back in one piece."

It was rather odd to fly for the long haul without anything to say along the way. The Great One seemed to know where he was flying. I believed we were flying west.

He made several stops until we reached the destination. Within seconds, I knew it was Moskwa. His eighth stop was on the rooftop of a flat. The building was bright enough to see where to walk but dark enough to hide any mischief.

With one pull, he opened the door of the emergency route. For fire, we had different escape systems than in Western countries. The layout of this building was puzzling to me. I wasn't familiar with this one, so I followed him instead.

In front of one door, I heard a woman sobbing inside. The Great One held the handle but paused after. As he was looking at me, he asked, "Are you ready, Nika? Because after this, your life will never be the same."

I nodded.

He opened the door and held it for me. He led me to Lyena in her small bathroom.

A pure one that the world could have. So beautiful. So vulnerable. But at the same time, he had a strong will to find his mother's nipple. He suckled with persistence to put away his hunger. He grabbed his mother's breast with his small hand, clinging to it.

Lyena, on the contrary, was covered in blood. Her life was hanging by a thread. Undead. There was no more life in her eyes. Yet we were grateful that she managed to feed the baby. She kept him alive until we arrived.

"He is mine."

She nodded without saying a word.

His cord was still intact, so I pulled out my knife to cut it. "We need to call someone." I was turning my face towards the Great One when I felt her hand on my wrist.

Lyena was practically drowning in the pool of her own blood. "He's doing me a favour, Kolya. You need to let me go. It's time."

"But he is—"

"He is your son. It's only been an hour, but he already showed your best traits. He has the best father he can ever have. Also the best uncles." She put the baby in my arms. He was so little compared to me. "You're both strong and gentle enough to raise him."

The Angel of Death drew his Light and walked into the bathroom. "You should wait outside. She's mine to take."

I did what I was told. Lyena might have prepared baby clothing or nappies for him. I tried to clean him as much as I could before giving him a nappy and a shirt. The trousers were still too big for him to wear, but I decided to put them on him anyway. He needed to be kept warm, so I gave him three layers of clothing. There was a clean bed sheet in the wardrobe. I cut it in half to wrap him around my chest with it. He could now snuggle under my suit.

The Great One watched me while leaning his side against the wall. "Considering her profession, there's a chance that he isn't yours. We have your DNA record, but I'll take some of yours, too, just in case." He cut some of the baby's hair and mine.

His sword was already sheathed behind his back, and his twelve wings were retracted. He was another father figure of mine. He took care of us, the orphans, in the most uncommon way. His wife was a mother figure who provided us with shelter, also in the most uncommon way.

When I looked at my watch, it was half past two in the morning. The baby got sleepy under the wrap. "Whose day is it, my Great One?"

"The feast was for Saint Ivan Rilski, the Patron of Bulgaria. Then it became the Day of People's Awakeners. So the celebration also goes to authors, educators, and the ones behind the revolutionary minds and movements."

I bowed to him. "Ivan Nikolaevich."

He kissed Vanya gently on the head. He tapped my arm, and he nodded before leaving the flat. My son and I were following behind him.

8

The Pact

Kolya

"Hristo, I'm in Moskwa. Can you get here?"

"Okay, what trouble are you in with the Great One?"

"It's, uh—"

I looked at Vanya, who was waking up to my voice. He was cooing and close to crying. "Shh." I tried calming him down.

"Well, after Samhain, if you can."

"We better celebrate it together, yes? I'm bringing the brothers with me, Kolyasha."

Hristofor Krastev stepped up to the role of being the man of the house when all of our fathers passed away. Just like his Bulgar father, Krastyo, he towered high with broad shoulders as he grew up. Being 193 cm in height, it was easier for him to pull our shirts from behind if we had fights than to yell at us. He always kept us rascals in good manners.

As the youngest and shortest one, most of the time I watched him keep orders in the family. Even though I was **12 cm** shorter than him, he always noticed if something went wrong with me.

He had the exceptional humility to learn anything new, even when our mentors chose me to be the leader of the Svyatoslavs. All six of us respected him so much for the way he kept our family together. I was to be the leader of our pact in completing projects, but Hristo was always the head of our family.

Vibrating.

"Kolya? Saint."

"Speak."

"The Great One told me to come to you. He said that I'm the closest one to reach you."

"I'll send you my location."

"Is the package all right? Anything you need?"

"The package's fine so far."

"Are you all right, *Brat'ya?*"

"I, uh, kind of don't know what to do."

"Aren't we all clueless? Hang in there, brother."

He hung up.

***

Kolya
Around a Decade Ago

I kept watching them through my scope, even after five hours of recon in the desert. The Din State rebellions had been in and out of their compound all day long.

There they were, and the women exited the compound to be transported elsewhere, no matter whether they were young or old. Their families either sold them or someone from the rebels abducted them for simply attending school. Then they turned them into slave wives for the rebels.

I would be slaving my future wife in bed, but not like those rebels. She would have a say in becoming my sex slave. The thought of me having a slave wife had come to my head many times. I was already wicked for even thinking about it.

I was about to take them down when a soldier appeared out of nowhere and slit the rebels' throats. *"Why would a soldier be alone for an operation like this? Is he lost or what?"*

His motive wasn't clear to me. But if he aimed for the same target, he could make my work easier.

With so many rebels coming his way, I cleared the ones around him. He looked in my direction for a few seconds before continuing to fight them.

"*Damn! Who is that man?*"

He had high skills in close range combat. He didn't even need to bring any weapons. He used his bare hands and the enemy's own weapons against them.

He was in a rage. There was something personal that he needed to burn down to ashes. He was doing his own shadow-work, fighting the inner battle he had in his chest or mind. I wondered what built him that way. I wondered what happened to him that awakened the beast inside of him. By clearing his way to free those women, I kept helping him from afar. That was until I felt a heavy hit on my head.

The next thing I knew was to wake up hanging upside down. Beside me was whom I assumed to be the rogue soldier. He, too, was hung upside down.

"Morning, sunshine. The princess slept all right?"

"Just the two of us? Where's your party at?"

"Yo, I got lost, brother. Where's yours?"

"They got lost, I think. Svyatoslav."

"Saint. I'd like to say that it was nice to meet you, but given the time and place, it's not nice."

His callsign was easy for me to remember. "Nice fight out there. Bet you got many medals already."

"Well, not everything I've done is something I'm proud of."

"Likewise, brother. We aren't Saints, in case you forgot."

"Damn right, we ain't no Saints."

***

Kolya

Saint was another orphan that I met a long time ago, when he was still serving in the Special Forces. He, too, had so many losses in his life. He just lost his fiancée to cancer a few weeks before I caught his act through my rifle scope. He was indeed lost at that time; I couldn't imagine the raging hell inside him.

When he and his wife first boarded Slava, I met Mandy in the library. Then I met Saint again after he completed his training and set foot in shadow-working. If we were to get another additional brother into the family, no doubt, I would vote for Saint.

He knocked on the door about three hours after the call. "I asked Mandy what to get. These are all I could find. Not many are open 24/7 on the way here."

"Appreciate that, Saint. This is Vanya."

"Maybe you can give him to me. I need to practise doing the daddy thing before mine arrives. Wifey barely passed the morning sickness phase."

"Congratulations. Here he is. You can practise with him."

"You should sleep, though. You look like shit."

About four hours after Saint came, my brothers arrived. Immediately after I opened the door, Klima said, "Where's my nephew?"

All my brothers except Hristo just barged in to meet Vanya. None of them even said 'hi' to me. "So, our baby brother became the first father in the family," Hristo said.

"You are no longer our favourite, Kolyasha. *Him*, the boss now," Klima said while holding my son.

He was my son. As weird as it was to say the word 'son,' we were blessed to welcome a newborn into our family.

9

Shelter

Alma

My door was opened. At the back of my head, I knew it was *him*. The air breezed his scent when he entered the room. At this point, I craved his presence. With my body facing the window, I laid still on my bed. I was restless, waiting for him.

"You've been here before. Supposedly, you know where everything is." From the sound of it, he must be restocking my refrigerator in my kitchenette. Tonight was different than usual; I knew it was him, but not entirely him. There was another scent that stung my nose.

"You should go back to sleep. I only need to lay down for a while." He laid himself behind my back. When he spooned me, the smell on top of his scent became recognisable to me. He caught me when I was rolling towards him.

"Please, I need to know who's been providing for me." Air was rushing in and out of my lungs rapidly. My heart was pounding faster, just like it wanted to break free from my rib cage.

We had never been this close. His hand kept my wrists restrained. "You don't need to know."

I was writhing only to get away from his restraint. To see him. To know him. To touch him. "But I want to know. Need. Whatever, please."

His growl vibrated on the side of my neck before rolling me to lay on my back. He hovered over me, keeping my wrists together. The rope almost came out of nowhere. He started tying my wrists and, after that, lacing my forearms together. "If you want to know so much, then watch. Watch who you belong to."

Wearing a dark single-breasted suit, he had a light colour shirt underneath it. A dark tie matched his suit and mask. He meticulously laced me with his rope. With the darkness of my place, I couldn't tell the colour of his eyes. They paid attention to the craft he made through the hole in his mask. There was something in those eyes that told me that I was safe with him.

When he was done with my forearms, he moved to my legs. He started by tying my ankles and lacing up my knees. He had my shins held closely. These lacing ropes provoked my arousal, and just like that, he commanded the wetness to leak out of my pussy.

Even if my forearms and legs were tied up, I knew that I'd be safe with him. "Mmh... please, Sir. Mercy."

After finishing his harnesses on me, he rolled me to the side. His arm slid underneath my neck, and finally, he pulled my body closer to him. "That's more likely. You should have begged earlier."

"You were away for months, almost the entire winter. Whose blood is it? I can smell it on you. Are you hurt, Sir?"

"Yeah, your bedsheet and blanket need to be washed tomorrow. But the blood isn't mine." He snorted, but no explanation came out of his mouth.

It felt surreal to be under his guard for real. I felt like gravitating towards him. I felt as if I was seeking refuge in his arms. "Thank you—" My tears started leaking down my face. "Thank you for the gifts under the pillow. And for providing for me. No one else sees me like you do."

"It's me taking care of you, Alma." He slid his hand under my t-shirt. Those fingertips of his started dancing on my belly. They moved down to where my womb sat. "If anyone else dares to take care of you, I'll break their necks. This one is mine."

I couldn't hold back my smile, as I had never known this possessive side of him. I didn't know him at all, but I knew that he was guarding me. "How was Christmas at your place?"

"Busy. The north is far more brutal than here."

"Do you like tying women like this?"

"Just you. Though I like freeing other women from it, I send them to Chur for refuge after."

Those words pounded into my chest. I wondered if I was simply an option for him. "If you have so many choices for women in Chur, why are you here?"

"Because you are my refuge, *Dusha Moya*." My name technically meant 'the soul.' But the way he gave me a name sounded different to me. Calling me 'his soul' like that made me feel like I mattered to him. But with that blood on his suit, I wondered if he was a person without a soul.

"*As you are mine, guard.*"

***

My legs were freed first. He rubbed the rope marks on my shins with care. Waking up to someone pouring kisses on my legs was fictional before this morning. Even through the fabric of his mask, I could feel his gentle care.

He then released each knot of what had harnessed my forearms for the entire night. Not much of the ray of light had brightened my place yet, but I could see him. There were remains of raging waves in his eyes, but there was also calming water when he looked at me straight in the eyes.

He was nocturnal. The eyebags were heavy under his slightly downturned eyes. Dawn might be his only warning to rest. He might be restless, even when he closed his eyes.

He caught my wrists when I was trying to reach his face. "Don't!"

"I only need to touch. Please."

His grip loosened, so I placed my hands on his masked face. He let me trace his features. My forefingers traced his straight nose. He didn't have excessively high cheekbones, but they were high enough to place my middle fingers higher than my ring fingers. His cheeks were not too hollow, but enough to create valleys for my ring fingers to be buried in.

My thumbs traced his lip lines until I found his lip corners. He didn't have extremely full lips, but my pussy should put away his starvation, and my arousal should wash out his thirst.

"How come you never asked for anything from me in return, guard?"

"I don't ask. I take."

Slowly, I lifted my blanket with one hand. "You know I don't have much. But please take everything

I have left." I pulled up my t-shirt with my other hand, freeing my bare breasts for him. It was me who starved for his touch.

10

Shelter

Kolya

The hand she used to trace my face was small compared to my hand. But that was my thought before she displayed the perfect menu for my breakfast. She made me salivate with those serving breasts. After I saw them, my hunger rushed in. She was clueless as to how long I had been salivating while watching her perky breasts from afar.

"I won't look if you don't want me to."

I pulled her t-shirt up until it covered her face. With her hands on top of it, I tied my rope to hold them together. Firm, but loose enough to keep her breathing for me. From now on, she breathed only for me.

My thumb traced her hardened nipples. I took off my mask before moving down to her breasts. These aroused nipples needed to be consumed thoroughly. They either belonged in my mouth or in my hands. One day, they belonged in our baby's mouth.

She let out a slight moan when she felt the scruff of my beard on her skin. "Sir, please, I need to touch you while you're taking me." She didn't get to touch me, not before she let herself go to me. She was still restrained. Her mind, her heart, and even her life, for being the middle ground of her family. She took the hit for everyone's sake but herself.

"These breasts are mine now. No one touches your body. Not even you without my permission."

"Understood, Sir. Just you."

When I peeled off her shorts and knickers, her arousal welcomed me. "You should see how tasty she looked! Drenched for me."

She widened her legs to let her glistening pussy welcome me home. Her pussy being fucked in any way possible would be the perfect gift for my good girl. But she needed to understand that I had many different forms of torture and punishment for her.

My fingers moved along her folds so slowly. Too slow, even for me. As much as it tortured me to move this slowly, I needed to torture her first. I gave her the lightest touch to her clit, while holding myself back. "Whose pussy is this now?"

"Yours, Sir." She let out a sigh of relief when I finally started feasting on her. She tasted just like I imagined—like a sweet, perfect breakfast.

"When I tell you to come, you come for me. Only for me. Your pleasure is for me." From now on, she would become all of my three meals. Breakfast, lunch, supper, and even the light bites in between—I would take her whenever my hunger struck.

"Mmm... Yes."

With two fingers inside of her, I could feel how close she was. "That's it, Alma. Come for your owner." I slid another finger into her to massage her walls thoroughly.

She sounded like she was crying out while releasing, but I knew it wasn't a sad one. Every essence of hers needed to be lapped clean. Every drop of her cum along the slit and on my fingers belonged to me. "That's my sweet girl. You gave me so much juice for breakfast."

Her hands were now free from the rope, so she could touch me. I fixed the rope so her t-shirt wouldn't fall off her face. "I'll only be generous this one time. After this, you'll become my slut."

"Thank you, Sir." Her touch was soft on my bare face; I let her take off my suit. While untying my tie, she asked, "Would you use this on me one day?"

"If you are being a good enough slut, I might." I continued where she left off, stripping myself naked, just like she was.

Her hands were exploring me anywhere she could reach me; I let them wander. She gasped when her hand found my cock. "Sir, I—"

"Yes, you *will* fit me. Now take all of me like a good slut, or I'll ram my cock all the way in." I lifted her thighs so she could hold my waist with her legs. Then I worked my way into her smooth tunnel. "That's my pussy, fits me so well. Who said my pussy wouldn't fit me?"

"Oh, I feel... so full." Her moan filled my ears just like music. She didn't feel tight or biting. She felt like melting into me, and then we became one without any end or beginning. She was close once more; I could feel her walls clenching.

I was so restraining myself from riding her rough, or I thought I was. I was a fool, thinking that I could hold myself back from her. "Give me another one, little spark. Burn me with your cum." My cock stroked just like a revving engine, speeding up to her finish line. Here, I crossed it, flying her checker flag for the second time.

"Time to throw away your pills before I tamper with your birth control myself."

While recovering from her orgasm, she said, "But I still have a few months in uni—"

Her response heated up my thrust. "Didn't I just make you my slut? You forgot your place already? Hmm?"

"No, Sir, I haven't forgotten."

"Good. I take this womb, too. To grow my babies." Spraying my cum inside of her, I claimed her as mine. "Now, you are mine, *Dusha Moya*." I put on my mask before taking the t-shirt off her face.

It felt right to have her in my arms all night. Everything came into its place when I cuddled her like this in the morning. It all made sense now. I had a sound mind when I was with her.

She listened to my heart beating for her. "I defended my thesis last month, but I took extra classes this semester. I, um, I didn't know how to get to you if I didn't prolong my stay here."

"I'll find my way to you, Alma."

She nodded. She was silent, calculating me. "What do I call you, guard?"

"Kolya."

"Hmm. He's the Patron of this city, Nikolai. But for Switzerland, it's St. Nicholas of Flüe."

"Glad to know that someone studied hard. That's my good girl, making me so proud. What do you want for the gift?"

She curled her body, sinking further down in my snuggle. "I already got one, right here."

While watching her eyelids get heavier, I could tell how much she resisted them from closing. Once she fell asleep, I then took a shower.

She was still sleeping when I finished showering. Her refrigerator and kitchenette were stocked now. There would be no excuse for her to skip any meals. She might think that I was unaware of her cutting her budget. It was my duty to know these things about her.

When preparing breakfast, I tried hard not to make so much noise. I didn't cook like a chef, but I knew how to, out of necessity. Before leaving her, I inhaled her hair through the fabric of my mask. "This body is mine now. Everything about you is mine. Take good care of my belongings, Alma."

Her hand pulled mine out and held it to her chest. "I will. When will you be coming here again?"

"As soon as I can. Don't wait until your breakfast gets cold."

"When you go, um, to do what you need to do... Please make it home to me, Kolenka." She kissed my hand, just like I were something precious to her.

"I can't promise you anything. I'll try."

She leaned her body towards me, craving another hug from me. "Do try, Sir. I'll be waiting for you to come home." She was my home now.

11

Diversion

Kolya

"Something isn't right. It smells fishy."

They weren't actually loyal to Yuren, but no doubt they were loyal to Yurena's cunt. She made each hole in her body a trophy. And they were loyal to her, competing with one another to impregnate her. Since she was the only one left of Yuren Bratva to see the day, whoever fucked her hard enough and got her pregnant would have the power to control her base and resources.

Yurena made it as a way of avenging her brother's death by going further than two steps ahead of us. She kept bettering her crew to work on suicidal missions and purposefully aimed to cheat death. Her crew kept getting better and better at disappearing from us in the sea. Thirteen women were transported on a disguised merchant ship. Mobhi traced them down for almost two days straight, relentlessly.

Every time he traced something or someone in the water, he seemed to be talking to the waves in the ocean, the wind in the air, and the stars in the sky. Indeed, the waves, the wind, and the stars seemed to be talking back and forth with him. On the third day, Mobhi intercepted their course, and then Klima took care of the merchant ship. He finally sank their ship in the Mediterranean Sea. The shadow-workers dove to fish those women out of the sea and brought them into our submarine.

Two days after that, we docked in Genoa. I got out of the submarine first. On my bike, I went to the higher ground ahead of the rest of them.

We transported those women on an RV, with Hristo and Kolman guarding them as the first layer. Kolman navigated in front of the RV. He prepared for alternate routes, while Hristo handled all the logistics for all projects. Most of the time, Hristo rode behind the RV.

Adya and Seva guarded them as the second layer. They rode and guarded the perimeter wherever the transportation was. Seva rode at the rear end to sweep off all tails. Adya rode near Kolman at the front to clear his route.

Dealing with the arms dealers, Adrian Romanov prepared all the weapons we needed for our projects. He actually prepared the weapons for most of the shadow-workers. Adya was always into details. Sometimes he modified or tailor-made them for projects with certain purposes. He could make a weapon out of nothing since we were young. Even though he didn't look like taking everything seriously with his sense of humour, he was always our protector. He saw threats much sooner than any of us. And for this project, he smelt it as much as I did.

From Genoa, we were to make a stop in Como. The Great One and his Legion of Watchers, built a base in Como after their Falling Day. In the present day, the base in Como remained a wall to guard Chur.

"*Lose my tail, Crown,*" Seva said.

"*I got you in sight. Can't blame them, Arrow, you thick.*"

"*I'll ring the bells, so everyone can sit on the carpet.*"

I watched them from the Castello Baradello, waiting for them to speed up. They were going towards the Cathedral of St. Mary Assunta, which famously had beautiful tapestries hanging.

Seva reduced his speed before splitting towards the Basilica of St. Abundius, which had notable bell towers. I kept watching him from above.

"*Crown, tail! My cake's itching.*"

I took down two of the tails before they could see where the group was going. "*What can I say? The* cake looks like begging for spanks. Bet they were tempted to have a piece of it."

Before Seva started complaining again, I cleared him from all of his chasers. "How's your thick cake feeling? Lighter now?"

"Hey, sprogs, can we regroup now? You two talked too much about cake. I'm starving here. Gotta run fast. I can already smell the fish," said Adya, as he shared the same suspicion with me.

"What? You want my cake, too, Butcher? Share with Crown, yes?"

Seva intercepted to regroup. They continued the roadmap, while I moved on to my next checkpoint to wait for them to pass. Then I moved to the checkpoint after that. I kept moving on to the next one until all of us reached Chur.

"Something's itching that I need to scratch. Something I can't tell what it is yet."

12

Taken

Kolya

All the tunnels underneath Switzerland were upgraded; the soil was to remain neutral. Some referred to it as the gate of hell, others as a robust contingency plan, and the rest as a shelter.

The bunker in Chur was built in ancient times. Now, it had also become a safe haven for the women who were trafficked. It was modernised for the operation of the institution. The women who sought refuge in Chur were given some time to retreat, heal, and recover. For some of them, it wasn't about physical weariness but emotional scars. Some started to move their bodies within days. Others took longer even to be able to speak a complete sentence.

Of all the facilities that the institution owned, Chur was the least visited by Milady. It wasn't because she didn't care about those women, but because some of those women were already pregnant when they came in. It could be dangerous for their newborns to be around Milady.

Before partnering with the institution, I assumed that trafficking only involved virgins and women with empty wombs. Little did I know that those traffickers made virgins and pregnant women their biggest commodities.

There was no place in my brain to fuck a pregnant woman carrying someone else's child. I imagined how fucked up traffickers' brains were. Without a doubt, I'd continue to fuck Alma when she got pregnant. But she was the woman I cared about, whose belly was swollen from growing *my* baby.

I kept tracking her, even when I was away. She made me feel so proud of her for passing all of her extra classes. I was so occupied with these projects and Vanya this entire spring. Months of not seeing her became a personal torture for my mind and my cock. The longer I went without drowning myself inside of her, the more I got messed up in my head. The less I flooded her tunnel with my seeds, the less patience I had in doing these projects. I needed to have her as soon as I could; otherwise, I'd lose my sanity.

At the same time, I was worried about her. We fucked once, but she hadn't seen me. I felt like she understood me, but she hadn't seen the truth about me. I wondered if the real me was too heavy for her to handle. I even wondered what she would think about someone with a child. The tests showed that Vanya was mine. Even without the test result, I knew that he was mine.

I wondered if my roles as a father and Watchman would give her enough reasons to leave me for good. Since the first time I saw her, I have always wanted to keep her in my life.

Vibrating.

"Speak."

"Kolya? Umm—" Her sobbing voice concerned me. Noises in the background concerned me even more. The most concerning thing was that I never gave her my number for her to call.

"Alma?"

"You want her alive; you come alone. No brothers."

"What makes you think I'd come?"

"Right. You took my brother. I'll take yours in exchange, starting from your delicate heart here."

"She's one of many stray girls that I found."

"Let me see if that's true, Kolyan," Yurena said. "You know where." She cut the call.

At that moment, I realised that those thirteen women we transported were a diversion. Immediately, I made my first call. The other end was picking up. "Saint, where's my bundle package?"

"Floating."

"Make sure it's secured. No leakage."

"Got it."

I hung up to make another call. "Hristo, I need you to lay low. This one is mine."

"Bundle package?"

"No."

"We'll trace her last location."

"What did you say?"

"Yes, yes, we know about the potential backpack. You should give up trying to get rid of us already. We're your brothers."

Almost barking, I said, "Hristo, it's Yurena. She's madness."

"I should lend you a mirror, then. I'll get back to you. Stay put. I mean it, Kolyasha." He hung up.

✳✳✳

My brothers would know that I wouldn't listen to them when it came to what I thought was right. Alma was important to me because I knew that she was the right one for me. And it was only right for me to come alone for her sake. My focus was on getting Alma free. So far, I only had one escape plan—nothing but an exchange of myself for her.

Yurena and her people wanted me, not Alma. They used her to get to me. They abducted her and kept her on Kotlin Island. They must had locked her inside of the old Fort Rif. That one was located in the deepest layer of guards.

Fort Konstantin was their first layer of walls. They welcomed me fully armed, as they should. They searched for my weapons but were surely disappointed because I brought nothing with me. I could be more dangerous when unarmed; their newbies didn't know that yet.

They transported me in a car to face their leader, Yurena. There were many surveillance forts in the south of Kotlin Island; Fort No. 3 Count Mlyutin, Fort Imperator Pavel I, Fort Alexander, Fort Pyotr I, Fort Konshlot, and more. They had another one in the east—Fort Porokhovoy.

On the north, they had nine fortresses to guard Kotlin Island; Fortress Obruchev, the First Northern Fort, continued until the Seventh Northern Fort. In the far north of the island, they had Fort Totleben; some called it Fort Pervomayskiy.

Kronshtadt used to be a naval base in Sankt-Peterburg. The name could mean the city of the crown. Also, it served as a base for sailors and naval soldiers who rebelled against the Bolsheviks. In the past, they considered the Bolsheviks to have failed to provide for the people. Yakornaya Square, in the heart of the island, had another name that meant the Square for the Victims of the Revolution.

On another occasion, I would have brought Alma to spend some time on Kotlin Island. She must have liked this Naval Cathedral of Sankt-Nikolai the Wonderworker. We would enjoy our secluded time together. With so many forts and prisons in the dungeons, I should be the one who held her captive. I would fuck her senseless in the dungeon until she begged me for more.

13

Escape Plan

Alma

I couldn't eat this breakfast. It wasn't because I was being a brat and not grateful for what they gave me. It was because my wrists were tied up too tightly; I almost couldn't feel my hands. I shouldn't even be tied up like this. Only Kolya deserved to tie me with his ropes, not them.

The way he tied me didn't feel like restraining. Instead, he made me feel that those ropes were extensions of his body. Each line and knot made me feel like he was hugging me. He made it firm, but not hurtful. There was no stinging tension that I felt from his ropes, only a gentle hold for me to snuggle.

We shouldn't meet this way after months of being away from each other. I missed his touch, even his scent. I missed sniffing his scent floating in the breeze. His aura was greying the air whenever he was around. The grey wasn't for blinding me; instead, it was for blinding them from ever finding me.

The moment the door was opened, I could immediately sense him. When his scent rushed into my lungs, my body absorbed his presence. From there, he grew my second skin to armour my soul. He made me feel secure, as though bullets couldn't pass through. The way he locked his eyes on mine told me that the armour fit me.

It was him—the one I met in front of the Cathedral. A half of me always wished that it was him, hoping that Kolya must be him. Even with his wrists tied, he was walking straight with his head held up. His lips weren't curving a smile when he saw me, but his blue eyes were. Those eyes were the calming water of the ocean, replenishing my soul.

As he walked towards me, I stood up from my chair. He gave me my new favourite necklace—the grip of his hand. With his dominating hand, he stretched my neck up to reach his lips. I parted my lips, craving his caressing touch. I'd take anything that I could consume from him after months without him inside of me.

After only a few moments of devouring my lips, he broke our kiss. "Get her out of here. I'll deal with my slut later." He took away my necklace. He didn't ask how I was doing. Nothing. He said nothing to me.

"Is it true that he sees me only as his slut?"

It was true that he had those other women in Chur. Foolish me for thinking I was someone different than simply another slut for him. He turned his face towards me and said, "I didn't have to deal with this mess if you were grateful enough. But you had the urge to be so curious about my work."

"I'm—I'm sorry, Sir. It won't happen again." It was true that I looked up some information about him—anything that could bring me closer to him after uni life, which was soon to be over.

I was trying to swallow the bitter reality of it. My tears were pooling in my eyes. It was true that he was the only one who deserved to make me cry, but not like this. I'd prefer him making me cry, whine, and beg for his mercy in bed. Not here in this way. I was wrong to hope for more than what was given to me.

"Wait outside," he said. Not a request or question, but simply an authoritative command.

I nodded and kept my eyes locked on the floor. "Yes, Sir." I couldn't hold back my tears any longer. They fell to the floor before I turned towards the door. My feet were swept heavily to follow the guards as they walked out of the room.

There was no more of his scent once I was outside; I started to smell the saltwater breeze. Then I tasted blood inside of my mouth—it came from something pointy and sharp that wasn't there before.

Kolya gave it to me when we kissed, but I didn't realise it. It was surprising to see his face without the mask on. I was so smitten that it clouded my judgement for survival.

He came for me. In there, he was also right. Although he made me his slut in bed, he cared for my needs beyond bed. He cared about me so much that he came here to get me. If I got his message right, he wanted me to free myself from this restraint. He needed me to run away from those guards.

14

Dust

Kolya

Yurena signalled her guards to keep their distance from us. Kotlin Island was indeed beautiful, regardless of how secluded it was. It was built for a specific purpose that needed seclusion to function. I came here alone, but I shouldn't be alone in here with Yurena.

Fort Rif would be perfect to keep the most dangerous prisoners. No one would dare to even think of a quest to free someone from this northwest fort. "So you made the restoration. Nice upgrades to the place."

"Thank you. Such an eye for detail. We upgraded the security, too. Do you like it, Kolyan?"

"I'd fuck someone in here."

"I heard you like to play with your prey. Captive? Ropes?"

"What now? You want to be my object?"

"You know, I'm the last Yurena. Those men I have are racing to get me pregnant every day. Sometimes they take turns playing nicely, but sometimes they don't." The thirty eight years old whispered in my ear, "I like it when they don't."

"And what's their reward? Your cunt?"

She started to kiss my neck and ear. "Yes, my cunt. With everything we buried in the womb of this island."

"That's tempting."

Her lips traced the scruff of my beard, moving to my lips. She shouldn't have kissed my lips; they belonged to Alma.

"I won't repeat myself again. Do you want to be my object?"

Yurena had no soul, just like I used to. "Too bad you are the one wearing the ropes. I like my man to be, let's say, handling the situation."

"I made cordage from nature since I was little, so of course I could free myself from this easily."

She was frozen for a few seconds, analysing whether she should call her guards or not.

With my now free hand, I pushed her against the wall by the throat. My other hand stopped her hand from reaching her holstered gun. "You don't know how to beg, do you? Dress off. Keep the high heels on." After taking her gun, I kept it behind my waist.

"Turn around." Her wrists were now tied behind her neck, making her elbows look like rabbit ears behind her head. I made loops around her forearms to keep them tied to her arms.

One of her guards came with his hand on the holster. "It's all right," she said.

"Actually, you can make yourself useful. Get me more ropes, long ones." I continued until the remaining end went around her chest.

Her guard came back with bundles of ropes. "This enough?"

"Bigger ones, but that'll do it." I paused, holding my laughter for his stare at Yurena. I bet he never saw her enjoying herself while tied up. "What? You want to join?"

"You can wait outside," Yurena said.

After finishing the ropes under the breasts and around the waist, I looked up to find a horizontal pillar that looked strong enough to support her body. I placed her under it, and then I threw the bigger rope. One end was tied to the loop on her upper back. Then, through the loop behind her waist, I slip through the other end.

"First time?" I pulled her up until her shoulders were higher than her waist. Fixing the bigger rope, I hung her body to lean forward at a 45 degrees angle. Her feet were elevated from the ground, but I didn't tie them together.

"Yeah."

"Glad I can be your first. You like it this way?" I locked the knot behind her waist so her feet couldn't reach forward towards me.

"Oh, you should see how my cunt likes it. She is already flowing like a river."

I move a step closer to her. With a tighter grip, I keep her still by the throat, facing me. "I'm more than glad to be your last. It's going to be your blood that flows next." Using her own gun, I sent a bullet straight to her forehead. Warm, fresh blood burst into my face.

"If you are to take someone's life, you do it the Rus way. Face them, so they can see the wave of fury raging in your eyes. That's your mercy on them," father said.

Immediately after the loud bang, her guards rushed into the room. Taking them down one by one, it was me alone against them. Changing from one gun to another, I kept them replaced and reloaded. Those dead guards wouldn't need any guns after all.

Even after Yurena was dead, her guards kept coming towards me. There must be something that the Yuren Bratva hid under this island that made the guards willing to fight for it. Yurena was the last one of her Bratva, so it became sort of a finder's keeper at this point. Without any leaders, they became mercenaries or even pirates for the treasure, whatever that treasure was.

It didn't distract me because I couldn't think of anything else other than Alma. The longer the two of us were here alone, the more dangerous it was for her. I needed to get her away from here as soon as possible. I kept moving towards the room where I left Alma before.

When she was no longer here, I shouted, looking for her. "Alma?" By calling her name, I summoned the guards as well.

"Kolenka?" She came out of a cabinet. She was indeed small enough to hide under there.

"She kissed me. I didn't. Though she should've asked you where to buy your lipstick."

"What?"

Those guards kept coming towards us, so I kept flying those bullets at them. "You know, the ones like yours. They don't stick to the skin. I like No. 286 more than the 224. It looks better on you."

She giggled at me.

"What?"

"Nothing. My stalker knows a lot about me. Ugh, there." She warned me about a guard coming from behind me. "I wouldn't know, Kolenka."

This one guard was persistent, while I ran out of bullets in my chamber. So I kept fighting and then choking him until he was out of breath. I took all of the weapons from the dead guards. "How come you don't know your lipstick?"

"Oh, I know my lipstick. I wouldn't know about hers if you didn't tell me. Your face and neck are covered in blood."

I touched the skin of my face. There was a stain of blood. "You're not scared of me?"

She shook her head. "I always feel safe when you're around."

"Can't kiss you with the blood on."

"Get us out of here, then you'll get more than a kiss."

"That one I agree on. You stay hidden behind me, yes?"

She did as I said as she followed me along. When we reached the front of the security room, she ducked behind my back. It would only jeopardise her safety even more to walk her outside blindly. To know where to go, I needed to see what was happening on the entire island.

"Stay here." I rubbed her cheek with my knuckles before going forward.

With a knife, I made a diversion to the far opposite side of her. It hit the stacks of their equipment. Two of them took the bait and left their posts. I took care of the other two inside of the room.

Once the room was cleared, I walked back outside to get Alma. Unless this time, they already had her. She looked calm, and that helped me a lot.

I asked, *"Сколько?"* ("How much?")

"Зачем?" ("How much for what?")

"За вашу лояльность?" ("How much to buy your loyalty?")

"По миллиону каждый." ("A million for each person.")

"Долларов?" ("In dollar?")

"Да." ("Yes.")

I eased my gun at them. *"Берегите дверь!"* ("You two watch outside.")

Once Alma was inside of the room, I called them. *"Эй! Пошол на хуй!"* ("Hey, guys! Go fuck yourselves!") I sent bullets to each of their heads.

"Kolenka? I thought—"

"What? I don't like them pointing guns at you." After picking up their guns, knives, and radio, I brought them inside. I then covered their remains.

She helped me move as many obstructions as we could find to secure the door. "That's rather sweet, actually." It felt wrong to love her giggles for this kind of reason. But she was adorable, no matter what.

I pulled her wrists; there were rope marks on them. "They tied you too tight, did they?" Kissing her wrists, I could only wish her bruises would go away.

"It's better now."

I picked one knife that wasn't too big for her hand. Once the sheath was secured, I placed it between her inviting breasts. "If anything happens, you have something to defend yourself with. But I'll make sure nothing bad happens to you." I didn't realise that she was staring at me with a gaze in her eyes.

"I remember you. Father Christmas delivers. Still don't think you should dye your hair white, though. You look hot this way."

"Only the good girl deserves her rewards. *After* we get out of here."

To make sure we had a clear path ahead, I switched the feed to another and another, and so on. While watching each feed from the cameras, I realised that the island and its fortresses still served their purpose as a base. Only the one who had power over them was different.

Wet and cold—that was what I felt when she wiped my face with a cloth. She must have found it around and then soaked it in the water. She continued cleaning my face and down to my neck. She was so nurturing. "Please, don't let me distract you. You look cute when you're making a serious face. I know that you're smart."

"I'm not cute."

"Oh, *I know* you're not cute. Hmm... what's your father's name, Kolenka?"

"Feofan."

"So, my maskman has a name, Nikolai Feofanovich. And which House are you from?"

"Svyatoslav." The sound of my name made her pause.

"I heard your family is like ghosts." She continued to clean my lips along with my chin. "It suits you, though. You watch me in the dark. There you are. I can kiss you now, yes?"

"Come here." A short kiss was all we could afford in this short amount of time.

"Ugh, the knife."

"It hurts you?" I repositioned the knife that I slipped under her bra.

"No. Just so you can touch the girls again. They missed their Daddy, you know," Alma said with her lips pouting. She became adorably annoying at this point with that bratty, whining voice. She surely knew her Daddy missed drowning himself inside of her.

"Back to work, Sir. You need to get us free from here." She made sure I did what she said.

"*What is that?*"

I tried to see it from a different angle. So that was it—the reason they became so persistent. That was what they hid underneath the island.

"Fuck! That's a lot."

There was something else I saw. In the water in the far northwest, that one, I knew down to the backbone of her.

15

Bush

Kolya

The radio comm was working all right, so I set the frequency to contact the sub-crew. "Svyat. Crown."

"Crown. Svyat. Anchor in command. Damn, I thought you didn't plan to pull the trigger. You know, getting too much in the mood. Yes, yes, I saw it. You okay?"

"Soul is with me. Bonfire here?"

"Standing by to light the fireworks. Northeast and south inbound."

"Catch us at S-1."

"Crown, that's far. You don't go crazy while the soul is with you," said Klima. That was the best trait that he had. He never hesitated to warn me, especially when I might be dangerous, even to myself.

"Not some news. Get the fireworks ready."

Since we were little, I knew that my brothers would always have my back. Yet, they trusted me to try it out first in my own wicked way. If it went right, they certainly celebrated even the smallest achievement. But if it went wrong, they'd be there—not to fix it, but rather to support me in fixing it. As soon as we found out that we had survived the mischief, all the banter was out. We'd be laughing at life itself.

"Alma, I need you to trust me on this. It isn't going to be a smooth ride out there."

"How can I help, Kolenka?"

She wanted to feel included and that she wasn't a burden to me. As much as I wanted to protect her, I couldn't do this alone at a time like this. So I showed her the way to reload the gun, and she even tried a few times. It was lovely to see how she paid attention; she always wanted to learn something new.

"This suit has bulletproof layers underneath." I put my suit on her. Once I was ready with weapons and comm, I cupped the face that framed her blushing cheeks. "I don't know how to say this—"

She held my forearms, assuring me. "I love you, too, Kolenka. You've been saying it since the stalking maskman came into my life. I'm ready."

We got out of the security room. I kept clearing our way ahead, and Alma kept supplying me with reloads. We didn't go towards the gate. Instead, we went to their garage to get a vehicle. There was no chance of coming out alive if we ran by foot.

The guards kept getting in our way. I didn't know such an orphan treasure could turn men so much into blood thirst. I figured that for the right amount of treasure, it could shift weak men into something else. Only the weak ones.

Once we reached the garage, I took every guard down. The exit doors were still locked. With this kind of terrain, a car would skid at chasing speed.

"Alma, wear a helmet." I took one of their motorcycles while she got the helmets for us. My backpack looked adorable when wearing a helmet. Not to mention wearing my suit, which was much bigger than her size.

"Will this fit you?"

"Yeah. Hop on."

She looked even more adorable when she struggled to get on the bike. "I'm sorry, how to—"

To help her, I got off the bike. "Hop on my back." I got on the bike again while carrying her. Officially, I got myself a tiny, adorable backpack.

I stopped near the button to open the garage door. "Press when you are ready," I said to her.

Once the door was open, they started firing. Then the chase began. While going as fast as I could to max the engine performance, I kept firing back once in a while. Getting far ahead was a better way than looking back to fire the bullets at them.

"I should have learnt how to fly one of those things a long time ago," I thought when we finally reached the airfield on the island. My best plan was to hijack an aircraft and abduct a pilot to fly it.

"Корона?" ("Crown?") A pilot recognised me after I took off the helmet. He just refuelled his four-seater aircraft. And then he saw the party behind us.

"Куда летаться?" ("Fly with me. Where to?")

"К С-1." ("Can you land us at S-1?")

"Ватрослав." ("Vatroslav.") He pushed his single engine aircraft.

"Очень Приятно. Она душа моя, Альма." ("Nice to meet you. That's my woman, Alma.")

I gave Alma a signal to board the plane before helping Vatroslav push it towards the bush airfield. He started the engine once we all boarded the plane.

Before setting his flap to 10 degrees at the beginning of the airfield, he made sure that Alma and I were ready. His engine was set to full power, and then he released the brake. His aircraft accelerated and was airborne.

"Что находится на С-1?" ("What's at S-1?")

"Моя подводная лодка. Чего?" ("My submarine. What are you thinking?")

"Связываетесь с ними по радио." ("Can you contact them on the radio?")

I set the frequency on his aircraft to contact Klima. "Svyat. Crown."

"Crown. Anchor. Go ahead. Wait, what's that sound?"

"We're in flight. The pilot wants to talk."

"Anchor. Firebird. I can fly and land near S-1 on the road. Or, maybe I can fly low enough while your submarine emerges. You follow my speed so I can drop the Crown and Soul. I will wave-off and continue flying after you submerge again."

"Have you done this before?"

"It will be an honour to have my first time over Svyat. One more thing, make sure the tall thing on your top is behind my plane tail. I need a clear path ahead."

"Crown, where did you find the mad pilot again?"

"At the bush airfield. You've heard the pilot. Conning tower behind his tail."

***

Kolya
10 Years Old

They just opened a new field for palm plantations. They needed to clear out the forest in order to start with their plan. Many natives and villagers had protested against the corporation. It was the sacred forest that needed to be sacrificed for the corporation's money and power.

Our mentors were the ones who protected the forest from harm. They did protect it to some extent. They did whatever they could to warn the natives when the corporation opened a new field. So that the villagers could stay away when the chopping, or worse, the fire, happened. The extent to which the government bodies were involved or how much their involvement in it was to be kept unknown for the sake of their advantage.

Just because the opening season ended didn't mean the loss stopped. The forest had died. There were obstacles from the forest remains and holes that could be dangerous for anyone who passed in the dark.

It cost us the lives of Feofan and Nonna. They sent me straight to an orphan life at ten years old. I had many father figures that would step up to the role of my father, but not of my mother.

She was our mother. She was the love that sheltered us together in warmth. My brothers and I wouldn't be the same children anymore. Our fathers had become widows.

"Help me bring their bodies onto the carriage."

Krastyo tried to stop me. "Nika, it'll be late soon."

"This land doesn't deserve their bodies. I'll find the place to burn them."

One of the seven mentors said, "We will watch from a distance. If he needs to do it alone, then he does it alone."

They helped carry my parents' remains. They brought me water and some food for the journey. I brought my knife, bow, and arrows. There went I on the carriage. Alone, I left my childhood behind.

After hours of journey, the night had fallen above me. The corporate workers stayed in two huts on the opposite side of the dead forest. There were still two people awake outside the huts.

I continued my carriage so no one would be suspicious of me. Since my parents came from a foreign land, my height wasn't the same as the natives' ten years olds. I parked somewhere secluded enough in the dark. While waiting for them to fall asleep, I filled the carriage with bushes until it towered high.

My cordage was already long, but not long enough yet. The moon had moved, so midnight must have passed. I waited for the moon to move a little more. When my cordage was more than enough, I brought them with me to the huts.

Once I was sure that everyone was asleep, I moved as quietly as the breeze of the wind. I tied the door handles and windows firmly. Each loop was secured with a knot. If anyone cut one string, it wouldn't open all the way.

I moved the carriage. The only hard thing was to make Kounrat silent. He could wake anyone up by making a noise. The horse belonged to the brave counsel of the mentors. After I placed the carriage in between the two huts, I walked him to a secure place. The huts were far away to hide their mischief from the villagers.

It started with two stones and bushes, then the small fire burned the tip of my arrow. I flew the fire to the roof of their huts. I kept firing them until there were only two arrows left. At last, I sent my gratitude—one for father and one for mother. From bushes to fire, and then to ashes. I was killing the small fire when the mentors approached in their tiger form.

"What? I said I'd find a place to burn them. I didn't say 'them' was only father and mother."

On Kounrat, I went back quickly to my brothers and other fathers. My mentors were running around me. There was a bird flying above us. I couldn't see what kind of bird it was, but I knew it was huge.

By the time I arrived, I knew that the fathers took turns waiting for me to return. My mentors roared to wake the others up. I hopped off the white horse near the fire.

The shifters then were no longer tigers. They were standing behind me until they moved beside me and turned around. They waited for the bird circling to land.

The bird didn't just drop and land in front of me. Instead, he approached at a constant angle that almost made him seem celestial with the shining sword in his hand. "Who is in leadership?"

"This youngest one. He's the only Svyatoslav left, our Great One," said one of the mentors.

He got down on one knee to level his eyes with mine. His sword shone like it was made of Light. "So one holy one has fallen into manhood. Let there be the House of Svyatoslav."

I looked at my mentors with questions and confusion about those words.

"Your training with us has been completed. You may return for another training if there is another lesson to learn."

"When the motherland calls, you answer. She has many tales to tell. You lead their way, youngling," the Great One said. When standing back up, he sheathed his sword behind his back.

So we left the foreign land to return to our Moist Mother Earth, for we were motherless children. My brothers kept the patronymics to respect their fathers. It was my family name that they had been wearing since then.

16

Salt

Kolya

"You need to pay attention to details, Nika. One big thing can break down because some small parts were misplaced or broken," Roman said.

I liked paying attention to details about people or their environment. I knew that I couldn't change people, but I could alter their surroundings. It was a rerouting, but most of the time it worked well in my world.

Kliment Romanov, being the youngest son of Roman, looked up to his older brothers, Adya and Seva. The three brothers got their interest in mechanicals and modifications from their father. He was meticulous with parts. It seemed like everything, big or small, could be modified in the hands of Roman.

Adya found interest in modifying weapons, while Seva found interest in modifying motorbikes. Klima was different from his brothers. He started by studying ships and then helped build Svyat. That was how he was familiar with Svyat through and through. He understood her more than I did. When she was whining, he called her *dorogaya* ("sweetheart"). And then she was all right again after he fixed her.

Klima was like combining the skills of his older brothers. The way he helped build Svyat was just like Seva's methods with motorbikes. The way he helped complete the submarine with her defence systems was something he learnt from Adya's thought process.

Klima would be in command each time I was on the road. He and I studied the same thing, but when it came to commanding, he gave her to me. He said that he could do the submarine but wasn't sure about commanding the crew.

***

"Crown, before getting out, set your seat fully backward so she can exit easily. Soul, stay on the back left, and then exit through the front right. Everyone understood?"

I looked back at Alma.

"Understood," she said.

Vatroslav requested that Svyat set her course against the wind while descending his aircraft to a lower altitude.

"*Svyat. Firebird. We have you in sight. Flying heading southwest,*" Vatroslav said on the radio.

Mobhi responded, "*Firebird. Voyage. Wind 215 degrees, speed variable at 13 to 15 knots. Altimeter setting 1009 millibar. Advise heading 215.*"

"*Altimeter set to 1009. Copied wind. Revise heading 215. Aircraft descending to 500 feet.*"

"*Turning to heading 215.*"

"*Reaching 500 feet. Airspeed 85 knots. Slowing flight.*"

"*Copied altitude and airspeed. Svyat is ready to emerge.*"

I pushed my seat fully backward and reclined it. Looking towards the back, I began to see Svyat coming out of the water.

"She's emerging," I said to Vatroslav.

"She's wide, isn't she? You have wide enough to hop on top of her?"

"Absolutely wide and thick, my sub is."

"*Firebird in sight. Aligning with Firebird's course. We're adjusting speed.*"

"*Descending to 150 feet. Intended airspeed 75 knots.*"

"*Copied intended altitude and airspeed.*"

"*Reaching 150 feet. Airspeed to 75 knots.*" He kept flying the aircraft, maintaining visuals of the aft of Svyat. *"Firebird on final descent to altitude 50 feet. Starboard exit."*

"Copied altitude and exit. Svyat is aligned with Firebird's course. Crown and Soul, you are cleared to board."

"Altitude 50 feet. Crown and Soul is offboarding."

He nodded towards me. *"Ни пуха ни пера."* ("Break a leg.")

"К чорту." ("To the hell we go.")

I got out of the aircraft first and then caught Alma. One of my crew members brought a rope for her to hold onto. She might be feeling wobbly if she wasn't used to it.

Once we boarded the submarine, she said, "Can I stay around you? Not too close, just to see where you are. I won't bother you, I promise."

I found her a seat in the corner of the control room. I imagined how she would feel if it was her first time. "I need to command. But I'm here." The crew handed me a blanket for Alma.

"Crown is ready to take over command."

"Your sub," Klima said.

"All stations. Svyat. Crown in command."

"Mothership copied."

"Pilgrim copied," Hristo said.

"Butcher copied."

I paused for a moment, thinking about whether we should call it a day or take back the power of the island, which is technically mine. I turned my face towards Alma.

"I'm still here," she said with a smile on her face. She was lacking sleep, I could tell. A part of me wanted to immediately bathe her and bring her to bed. Another part of me needed to put this conflict to an end. Then I turned to look around at my crew members.

Klima grinned. "I know your face when you're up to some mischief. Anchor is operative, whatever that is in your brain."

Mobhi chuckled. "Oooh, the backpack here needs to witness at least one of your mischiefs. Voyage is operative. Where to, Crown?"

"All stations. Crown. I took out their leader when Yurena was the last one of her kind. Let's take back the city of the crown, the entire island, and its fortresses. We don't do it for me. We do it for the rebel sailors and soldiers who have fallen on that bloody island. Keep the Church and archive untouched."

"Pilgrim is operative."

"Butcher is operative."

"Arrow is operative," Seva said.

"Celtic is operative," Kolman said.

"Firebird copied. Long range tank. Endurance 6 hours. I can be your eyes in the sky. Crown Senior helped my parents with food. We didn't have much when I was little. Like senior, like junior. That's how I recognised you earlier."

I nodded at Klima and Mobhi. "All stations, all stations, all stations. Firebird is operative."

"Firebird is operative," Vatroslav responded.

"Firebird, welcome to the big boys' club," Adya said.

"Mothership is standing by for refuge," said the captain of Slava.

I responded, "Svyat is standing by for the horn."

17

The Base

Kolya

After we turned our submarine around, we set our course to take Fort Rif, Fort Obruchev, and Fort Totleben. Once we were approaching Fort Rif, Svyat reemerged on the surface. "Get ready to broadcast."

"*Firebird. Crown. We need eyes over Fort Rif.*"

"*Wilco*," Vatroslav replied to comply.

Kolman remotely played the recorded sound of the carnyx, and we broadcast the sound of the ancient Celtic war horn. Our brothers and shadow-workers on motorbikes and cars were broadcasting the same sound from their vehicles. The sound was to mark the start of our fight. Hopefully, it would send chills down the opponents' spines.

"Snipers on starboard! Clean shots only." We opened the windows for the snipers to fire, keeping the starboard facing towards Fort Rif. When the sound of the carnyx stopped, I commanded on the frequency, "*Fire!*"

There couldn't be so many of their guards left inside of Fort Rif since I took more than half of them earlier on the ground. Our snipers continued to take down anyone left who kept firing from it.

"*Crown. Butcher. North Seven is taken.*" The typical Adya always called his work efficient. I'd prefer to call his work cutting through the bullshit. He didn't like to mess around or play with his food. That way, he was the opposite of me.

"*Crown copied. Open S-2 for us.*"

"*Crown. Firebird. Opponents fleeing out of Fort Rif.*"

"*Crown copied. Proceed to Obruchev and report.*"

"*Firebird is proceeding to Obruchev.*"

We waited for a few minutes, making sure that no one was firing at our sub anymore. And then I saw the flag that hadn't flown since the revolution.

We proceeded to Fort Obruchev to take over after Fort Rif.

"*Crown. S-2 is opened and locked. Butcher is proceeding to the North Three.*"

"*Crown copied. Pilgrim. Status?*"

"*Pilgrim is still working on Konstantin. S-1 is opened for you.*"

"*Ooo, the old man's getting slow,*" said Adya, joking with Hristo.

Klima joined the other snipers, leaving me and Mobhi in the control room to navigate from one fort to the next. "Approaching Obruchev. Snipers on port. Fire at your discretion."

"*Crown. Pilgrim. Konstantin is taken. Proceeding to the Kronshtadt.*"

"*Crown copied.*" The bulletproof Svyat would stand the attack from our opponents while our snipers kept firing. We heard the bangs over and over until it became silent.

"*Crown. Firebird. The Imperial flag's flying over Obruchev.*"

"*Crown copied. Proceed to Totleben.*"

"*Firebird is proceeding to Totleben.*"

"Snipers on starboard. Approaching Totleben. Snipers' discretion."

"*Crown. Butcher. North Three is taken. Proceeding to North One.*"

"*Crown copied.*" The snipers on board started the fire. Mobhi looked at me, waiting for my next command. His facial expression showed me that he was itching to pull the trigger himself.

"Mobhi, go around Totleben. We fire from the other side of the island."

"Aye." He set the course for the sub.

Once our starboard was facing the island, the snipers fired again. It felt like we'd been firing for hours by now. And then there was silence. "Crown, they stopped firing. Why did they stop?"

"*Crown. Pilgrim. Kronshtadt is taken. I say again, Kronshtadt is taken.*"

Then I saw the white-blue-red and yellow square at the top inner corner of it. The black imperial coat of arms inside the yellow square was the traditional one. It was flown at the highest point of Fort Totleben.

"*Crown. Firebird. All fortresses are flying the Imperial flags.*"

"*Crown copied. All stations, stand by.*"

"Mobhi, go around Kotlin, but stay close to the shore. Let the people see us."

Klima re-entered the control room.

"*All stations. Crown. We do not take prisoners. We do not offer any money. Ask them where their loyalties are.*"

Hristo asked through the frequency, "*Then where do you lay your loyalty, Crown?*"

"*Мать Сыра Земля.*" ("To the Moist Mother Earth.") When we decided to be loyal to the motherland, we served her people and the family who built a home in the motherland.

"*Then we follow the Crown.*"

"Anchor, your sub."

"My command," said Klima.

While cupping Alma's face, I kissed her on the forehead. "I need to go outside. Are you okay waiting here?"

She took off my suit and gave it to me. "I'm all right. You need to look good when they see you. Give them hope for the better. No tie, so they can see how approachable you are." She helped me untie my tie and unbutton two.

I went outside through the hatch. The sub crossed the ring road through S-2. We continued to go around the island. Through the monoculars, I could see people gathering at Petrovsky Park.

"Fly the flag," I said to one of the crew members who followed me outside. It felt wholesome to see them cheering to see the flag once more. The soil of Kotlin had absorbed so much blood a long time ago, as it did today.

The rest of the fortresses on the southern islands were also flying the flag. Then I told the crew members to return inside. I looked at the island one more time before closing the hatch.

"My command." I nodded to Klima.

"*Mothership. Crown. Children are coming home.*"

"*Mothership copied. We'll prepare supper. Borsh with yoghurt will be ready when you arrive. Pork or beef?*"

"Beef. With black bread if you have."

As soon as we established survival from the worst, the typical Adya started throwing banter, "Ooo, someone's going native. Crown be homesick now?"

Seva replied, "Fam, I don't want no beef with the Crown. Mother, Arrow gonna have the borsh with pork, yeah?"

The rest of my brothers bantered back and forth, and then I once again became their youngest one. I kept listening to my older ones until Hristo put them to rest once they became unfocused.

18

Mothership

Alma

There was a bumping motion as if this submarine was being caught with a giant claw. I didn't know how to describe it. I had no clue what it was called. It felt that we were no longer moving on our own. Something had been carrying us since, but we were still moving underwater.

Kolya said, *"Svyat is ready to enter the house. Mother, you have control."*

"Latch is secured. My sub. I have control," said the voice on the radio. The submarine was now being lifted.

"Svyat inside."

"Permission to board, Captain?"

"Granted. Hatches may be opened. Welcome home, children," said the captain, greeting us.

Kolya nodded to his brother and gave him a tap on the arm. "Klima, take it from here." He walked towards me.

I didn't realise how deep I sank into the corner until he lowered himself in front of me. Until his hands cupped mine, I held the handles so tightly; even my entire body was frozen tight. He made me feel safe. In his own way, he always told me that I could trust him. "You can hold my hands now, *Dusha Moya*." He kissed the backs of my hands gently.

"Um, Kolya, I was—I was drowning when I was little. I'm sor—"

"It's all right. Just hold my hands. No need to be sorry. We'll get out when you're ready. I should be the last to leave anyway."

He helped me rise when I started opening my body. His smile made me realise how tightly I curled my body like a terrified child. He walked backwards to lead me out of the submarine.

Once we were near the ladder, he pulled me closer. He hugged me tightly in his arms, just like he wasn't letting me go ever again. "I'm only a few steps after you. You trust me, yes?"

I nodded to him. I climbed a couple of steps and paused to look downward at Kolya.

"That's my good girl. Go on. Keep climbing."

By doing as he told me to, I was almost reaching the hatch. I looked downward one more time.

"That's it. You are close, *Dusha Moya*." There was something about the way he said those words that made my leakage unsealed. He said those words directly to my pussy.

"I got this," I said to a man who handed me some help. I went through the hatch by myself. On top of the submarine, I was on my knees at first, then I stood up on my own.

The submarine had become a part of the big ship. "SLAVA DECK -1," it said on the placard. Kolya walked beside me when boarding the ship from underneath. He whispered in my ear, "You make me feel so proud. My good girl deserves some rewards. As I said on the island, I'd deal with my slut later."

Everyone on this ship knew him. Wherever he walked, there was someone bowing to him or giving him a curtsy. He must be someone important here, so I kept my head down along the way. Once we reached the stairs with only the two of us, he turned his face towards me. "You are with me, *Dusha Moya*."

"I know. I can see everyone here respects you highly, but I'm a nobody here."

"Tell me, Alma, what are you to me?"

"I'm yours."

"That's right. You're my slut whenever you and I are alone. Out here, you hold your head up high. Show them that you're mine, so no one dares to touch my slut. Understood?"

"Understood, Sir."

We walked towards a massive medical centre, but not once did he release my hand from his grip. Only when we found the doctor and her nurses did he let go of me. "I need to be examined. You, too. After that, you get something to eat."

I nodded before watching him leave me. While listening to what the doctor explained, I watched her tools and equipment on the table.

"This is a standard procedure for everyone onboarding, except for the guests. We shall take samples of blood and saliva from you. Try to relax," the doctor said.

"It's been long since I had my last checkup, about two years ago, when I applied for a scholarship."

She asked me if I had any drug or food allergies. And then she asked about my last period and birth control. I was religiously taking my birth control pills until Kolya told me not to. Only after our first sex did he babytalk me. After about two months of not seeing him, I started to take my birth control pills again. I wanted to have a family, but with the distance, I thought he was ghosting me after sex.

I hadn't taken any since I was abducted. Now that we saw each other again, I wondered how he'd think about me disobeying him.

After the doctor finished with the examination, a ship crew came to me. He handed me a key to a Watchman suite on Deck 10. He put the medium size duffel bag inside of the suite, then showed me the way to the restaurant to have something to eat.

I was eating my supper slowly when Kolya came to the table. He fingercombed my hair. "I told you to take care of what belongs to me. You take care of yourself because this one is mine."

"I will, Sir. I just need to adjust. You know, in case I get sea sickness. Besides, I was waiting for you. We haven't seen each other for months. Anything I can get you?"

"They prepare some Borsh, but you can choose anything for me. I'll eat whatever you serve me." He kissed my lips gently. Then his lips moved to my ear, and he whispered, "These breasts and pussy are also on my menu."

His words controlled my body's reaction. My pussy was already drenched by now. Although I was sure that I would be his meal later, I left the table to prepare some real food for him to eat.

I needed to find out what he liked to eat and didn't, so that I could cook for him. But for now, we had our first meal together. That was enough for me after months of not seeing him.

19

Washout

Kolya

Other women I met might fall because of the bike I rode, or the suit I wore, or even the tattoos armouring my muscles. But she saw me pass through the layers of my guard.

Of all, my helmet was the only one that knew all the thoughts floating in my mind that had never been vented out through words. It absorbed the condensation from the raging hell inside of my brain. When the speed increased, the noise inside of my head went silent. Not everyone understood how speed affected the soul—that was, if I ever had any. Alma was the soul I never thought I had.

"Kolenka, is that you?" She only finished showering when I came after the crew debriefing.

"It's me, *Dusha Moya.*"

She smelt like home to me. She got out of the bathroom wrapped only in a towel. Her hair was cleaned and dried. It felt smooth when I nestled my fingers between her strains. "They gave me some clothes in the duffel bag. I haven't unpacked it. I'm sorry. I needed to shower so much. My hair was sticky."

"You don't need any clothes tonight." Her face was blushing. She looked innocent that way, but I knew she wasn't; the hell on earth forged her skin into solid armour. It was her brain that became the lethal weapon.

"I need to get a quick shower. Wait for me in bed."

"Don't get too long, Sir." She unwrapped the towel and walked naked towards her side of our bed.

The water washed out the blood and dirt that stuck on me. I watched it turn from clear to a reddish brown. The wind of the sea mixed salt and dust together. The breeze stuck weirdly to the skin, even stickier on me by wearing a suit.

The thing with Alma was getting real. This time, I wanted her to stick with me. I wanted *me* to stick with her, but I was stuck with my roles.

I needed to keep leading my brothers to watch over the seafarers on the salt water and deliver those refugees through the dusty ground. By fulfilling those roles, I gained opponents. My mind couldn't get rid of the thought that I almost lost her today. Someone else, like Yurena, wouldn't mind making her a target. Someone could be using her again to get to me. She wouldn't be collateral damage to me. She'd be a great loss if that happened.

It got me thinking about whether I should let her go. She was all right before she knew me. My Alma would definitely survive the world with her intelligence and work ethic.

With her kindness and beauty, someone would surely wed her. A peaceful home full of children would suit her. I would find my peace seeing her happily ever after, even without me in it. I loved her enough to let her go. But still, I'd slit open her husband's neck if he ever hurt her.

I already had Vanya to continue my legacy. My son was never her responsibility. It wouldn't be fair to ask her to love him as her own to begin with.

"You told me to wait in bed. And you said that I wouldn't need any clothes tonight." With her whining voice, she asked, "So why is the towel still hanging on your hips?"

Leaning on the door frame of the bathroom, I watched her adorable features with her pouting lips. I would keep her in my mind even after she went. Of course, I would continue to guard her as my precious one from afar.

"Because I just realised that I can't let anyone take you like that again. Or worse, harm you. It could be dangerous for you to be with me."

"What does it mean? Kolya, what are you saying?"

"You can have the bed for yourself. Once the ship ports in a safer place, you can go. I'll keep watching you from afar, as I always do."

"What if I don't want to go?"

"What if I want you to go?"

"Do you—do you want me to go?" She waited for my truth. "Kolya, do you want me to go?"

"I want you to find someone who can build a safe home with you." The tears were already pooling in her eyes. "Tomorrow, I'll ask them if you can have a new identity."

She rose from the bed. "Alma Hansdotter Svyatoslava. That's the new identity that *I want*, in case you're wondering about my decision."

"I'll sleep on the sofa."

She pulled the bedcover with her. Tears had fallen from her nurturing eyes. "Don't bother. You don't want me in your bed if you don't want me in your life."

I pulled her by the hair when she was walking out of the bedroom. "Don't push it, Alma."

"You are the one pushing me away. Don't blame me only because you felt helpless when they abducted me." Again, she saw me pass through my last guard.

"It wasn't your brothers or anyone else. It was you who took back the entire base. You have no clue how powerful you are, Kolya. Proof me wrong!"

That was it. She was the one naked, but I was the one being stripped down to my naked truth. No more shields. No more armour to guard me. Not even a mask to cover. There was no going back from this nakedness.

20

Diamonds

Alma

He stopped me by pulling my hair. He kept
me standing still. He didn't say anything back.
Anticipating—he was good at it. Even without him
wearing his mask, I couldn't read him.

His eyes were no longer like calming water. They
turned into raging storms, colliding with the waves
in the blue ocean. His chest was racing against his
emotions. He went back to reality when I rested my
hand on his muscular, hairy chest.

He wasn't like an ancient caveman pulling the
woman's hair. He was cupping the back of my head
while burying his finger between my hair. And then
he led me towards where he wanted me to be.
He put me in the place where I belong—under his
leadership.

Bundles of ropes were out of the drawers. He put it
around my neck loosely and made five knots in the
front. One knot between my clavicles, one between
my breasts, one near my waist, one near my navel,
and another one on my lower abdomen.

"Kolya, please say something."

"Turn around," he said. He pulled the remaining length through the gap between my legs. He connected the ropes with the loop line behind my neck. "Face the mirror."

He was meticulous with his craft. He worked the ropes around my body. He made what looked like diamonds in between each knot in the front. He connected each line with the one on my back. He divided each tension with knots at the back.

I touched the lines and knots he made. I could feel him hugging me through his ropes. It almost felt like he wanted to make me look beautiful with these ropes. His craft was beautiful on my body.

There were three diamonds. He was working on another one; the fourth one took him a while. He glanced a few times through the mirror. The raging wave of eyes caught me looking at the reflection of his craft. The harness started to look like a cozzy. He was armouring my soul to keep me from falling apart.

"It's beautiful."

"Let me see," Kolya said when he finished harnessing me. He checked each knot on my front side. He caressed my skin in between the ropes. Every friction from his touch against my skin ignited my core.

His hand started by cupping my jaw, then moved down to give me my necklace. "The next time you're about to cry, make sure my cock is choking this throat."

"Then let me have you."

He unwrapped the towel from his hips. "Down."

While stroking his length, I licked his tip and curled his head with my tongue.

"Stop playing with your food. Swallow." He held my head still while his cock thrust deeply into my throat. "Can't really say much, can you? Make sure it's 'Yes, Sir,' when you want to talk back to me."

He fucked my face to remind me that I was his property. When I gagged around him, he pulled himself out of me. "That's the right way for you to drop some tears. So beautiful. Now get your tongue out."

Messy. I was already a mess before he came into my life. He made me a lot messier by the way he fucked my throat. My pussy was already wet before, but now my chin, neck, and chest were slick from my own drool. By another gag, my face became wetter from tears.

He lifted me from my knees, only to throw me on his bed. It was he who licked all the tears that ran down my face. But the rush of his emotions was the one that consumed me. He relished my swollen lips, just like he was held captive without meals for days.

His lips traced down my neck, and he continued on my breasts. He took his time between lapping each of my nipples and squeezing them with his hands. He craved me as much as I craved for him to feast on me.

His lips moved further down, and he kissed my skin in between the harness he made. When his lips reached my folds, those eyes with the raging waves looked at me straight in the eyes. They weren't asking for permission, but telling me who my pussy belonged to.

He was so good at having my pussy as his meal and drinking my arousal that I needed to grip his forearms so I wouldn't be drunk on his passion. In a quick move, he released himself from my grips. Then he placed my hands in between his hands and my breasts. He led me to pleasure my own breasts.

That was what he did best. He didn't talk much. His movement was silent but loud, commanding my body. While my breasts were in our hands, his tongue commanded my pussy to release the wave of pleasure. And just like that, my body followed his lead.

I was recovering when he moved up to kiss me. When our lips consumed each other, I tasted my own orgasm on him. There were no longer raging waves, only the calm water of the deep blue ocean in his eyes.

"Tell me to go, and I shall be gone for good. You shall be dead to me and no longer be a part of my life. But I'm going to stay if you ask me to be yours." Underneath him, I started to cry once again. "Where do you want me? Tell me, and I shall obey."

"You are mine, *Dusha Moya*. Stay."

"Then I shall stay." I felt him planting himself all the way in between my walls. "Mmh... You are home, Sir."

With his thrusts, he was rocking my fortress and collapsing its walls. Here I was, taking shelter under my patron's flesh. Here I was, seeking refuge under the blanket of his scent. Under his patronage, I received the warmth of his mercy when he released his seeds inside of me to grow.

"Ich habe mich in dich verliebt, und du bist mir wichtig." ("I've fallen in love with you and you are important to me.")

He kissed me so gently, as if he didn't want to melt me because I was so delicate. He indeed melted me into him when he said, *"Oh, Alma, du bist die Liebe meines Lebens."* ("Oh, Alma, you are the love of my life.")

The safety of a refuge—that was what I felt while sobbing under his shelter. "Don't you ever dismiss me again, Kolenka." He cradled me for the rest of the night until I fell asleep in his arms.

21

A Place Called Home

Alma

Kolya told me to have my breakfast at the restaurant. He told me that he needed to get someone first. His family would join the table to have breakfast with us. His second breakfast, to be precise, because my pussy was his first one earlier today.

When he was walking towards the table, I could see who he was getting. "Alma, I want you to meet someone important to me. This is Vanya, my son." He was probably seven to nine months old, but I could see their resemblance. "I didn't know about him until he was born. His mother was gone after giving birth to him."

When my hands embraced him, he leaned his tiny body towards me. He hugged me back when I hugged him.

"He is my son, too." There was solace in Kolya when I said it.

Vanya reached for a slice of apple in my fruit bowl. "Can I get you something to eat?"

"Oh, he eats a *lot*. He can't stop chewing everything."

"Owh... Did you hear that, Vanka? Papa's getting jealous because I'll be *spoiling* you rotten." I handed another slice of apple to his little hand.

"What about you? Can I get you something, Kolenka?"

"Don't start teasing. I'll take everything from you."

While pretending to gasp, I covered Vanya's ears. "Language. We have a minor listening."

We spent the entire day making adjustments. Motherhood was something new for me to learn. I helped raise my sister when my mother started to work again, but it wasn't the same. Even when I taught my students as a kindergarten teacher, that, too, wasn't the same.

One thing I didn't know about his family was that they were seeking refuge in a foreign land. It made sense how he cooked once he told me that he grew up in a forest. He peeled and cut everything with a knife in his hand; no cutting board was needed. All the ingredients went into one pot.

We actually cooked in a similar way. We didn't grow up with much when we were little, so our family sort of cooked from what we had that day.

We made the most of what was available to us. That way, we grew up being grateful.

Kolya was right that I needed to find someone who could build a safe home with me. He was wrong about me needing to find someone else other than him. He gave me a family; I knew now where the word 'home' took place.

Vanya used to stay with someone who watched over him when Kolya went doing projects. I meant it when I said that he was my son as well. So I insisted on having Vanya live with us. Our little one had not walked yet, so he kept dragging himself to follow me. When I couldn't find a time to shower, Kolya said, "It's all right to ask for help, Mama."

I couldn't be more grateful for Kolya and everything he had been providing for me since the first time we met. Not once in my mind could I ever imagine having what we had. Everyone else was assigned a suite or a quarter when they boarded the ship, but not the Svyatoslavs. They kept dedicated leaders' suites on Slava.

"Maybe I should carry him. You might be occupied with the meeting with your brothers and colleagues."

"Are you getting attached to him, or so you wouldn't get nervous? I know it's a big family."

His thumb and forefinger pushed my jaws up to reach for his lips. The rest of his hand held my neck in place. I felt more intimate with him when he kissed me this way. Not that I didn't enjoy being fucked, but it was different. Different good.

"Why don't I carry him so you can relax a bit? You can carry him again when you start to get nervous."

We were scheduled to attend supper in a private restaurant on Deck 9. Kolya said that it was also to celebrate his colleagues' wedding and another couple's baby shower. That made sense to have one supper to celebrate more than one occasion since the Svyatoslavs were constantly moving around.

All of his brothers would be attending the supper as well. Two of them were on the submarine, so I knew what they looked like. Kolya showed me pictures of them together. He told me their names and their fathers' names. There was still a part of me that was nervous about calling them by the wrong name.

His brothers had always been solid ground for Kolya, so I didn't want to be such a disappointment. I knew that we came from different cultures, but I truly wanted to be a part of his life. Although I majored in Slavic studies, it never meant I knew everything.

Adya said, "Finally, the baby got a backpack!

"This is Alma. You know her already."

"Thanks for scaring the shit out of him."

Kolya turned his face towards me and said, "Alma, you know the boys, but you haven't met Natasha. She's Adya's wife."

"It's nice to meet you, Natasha."

"I'd like to say 'Welcome to the family,' but it's more of a jungle full of tigers here."

"But tigers protect the Sumatran forest, or so I've heard. I wouldn't mind, though."

"Ooh, it's nice to find another bookworm, innit? You must be Alma." The pregnant woman embraced me warmly. "I'm Mandy. This is Max, my husband."

"Welcome onboard. People here call me Saint." Vanya was obviously distracting Saint. "Eeey... where's my nephew? You missed Tio, no?"

"It's all right. He needs to practise daddying."

"When is your due date?"

"I'm almost thirty eight weeks now. The doctor said it's a boy. I already look like a hippo, but I still feel hungry all the time." She left me straight to the serving table.

"Ay, princessa, I like my hippo thick. I love my meat chewy like this," Saint teased his pregnant wife.

Following Mandy to the table, I took some for Vanya to eat. Kolya was right that Vanya liked to eat. He wasn't a picky eater, just like his father. The only thing was that I became his father's meal.

The newlyweds had come to join us. They greeted me at the table since I was feeding Vanya. I was a bit lost as to who was married to whom. Or maybe I was completely unaware that they were actually the captain of the next duty rotation with her three deck crews.

I was wiping Vanya's face and hands when the door opened. The hair on my entire body suddenly rose when I saw the tall, huge man who entered the room. He walked straight towards me and Vanya.

"Oh, shit. It's the man from the past."

When he was getting closer, I rose from my chair. My chest suddenly felt suffocated. Carrying Vanya, I walked backwards until there was no longer a space, and my back hit the wall behind me.

"Please don't hurt him!" I turned around to face the wall, covering his tiny body tightly with mine.

22

Reunion

Kolya

"That's my future wife, right there."

She curled her body to protect Vanya from what she thought was harmful. She covered him spontaneously, begging that no one would hurt my son. At that very moment, I realised that she meant it when she said that Vanya was her son.

"Vanyusha," the Great One said. The twelve wings were expanded.

Vanya laughed when he heard the voice. Alma seemed to be confused as to why he recognised the voice. She asked the Angel of Death over her shoulder. "You aren't going to take him, are you?"

"Of course, I'm going to take him. He loves playing with my wings." Our Great One reached out to take Vanya from her.

"Kolenka?" She asked for my permission to hand him over.

"It's all right. We were there together right after he was born."

"Ooo, what did you eat? You're much bigger already. You see that, Vanyusha? Mama remembers me."

Vanya giggled, playing with the feathers of the Angel's wings. To my innocent son, he was simply a guardian Angel. To the rest of the world, the Great One could be everything else.

"I remember your grandfather, Alma. I also remember your tiny body hiding in the wardrobe. But let's pretend that I didn't realise you were watching through the gap."

"So Vanya isn't—"

"The innocent ones aren't mine to take. Only this one enjoys taking more feathers than what he needs from me."

"I see no introduction is needed," I said.

"I see you took the shot to introduce yourself to her in the Cathedral. Otherwise, it would be worthless to send you to the archive in St. Nicholas. Though I can't recall taking Cupid's Duty to throw arrows."

"My Great One?" I made sure I heard him right.

"Well, I needed to keep track of her. Well, actually, if this one is nowhere to be found, she might be hiding in the wardrobe. Fortunately, I didn't have to do that much with the scholarship. Her portfolio spoke for itself."

"Pardon me?" Alma seemed a lot more confused than before.

"Huft, this youngling needed to move on and get his dick wet. This one didn't know when to get out of her situation. It was about time you quit becoming a referee for the family. What other excuse did you have back then?"

"I—I don't know what to say. Thank you, um, for watching over—"

"No. Thank you. If it wasn't for you, he wouldn't take back the base. This one, he needs a push sometimes." Milady held up Alma's jaws in her palm. She looked like she was examining her expression. "Hmm... his one doesn't know how powerful she is."

"Oh, Milady, she said *exactly that* to me last night. In an angrier way. Not in a good way."

"Interesting." Milady looked at the both of us in turns. "You two might be twins."

"We don't have the same parents, Milady," Alma said in a witty way.

"Ugh, those younglings nowadays, they lightly say, 'Oh, he's my twin flame,' without understanding what it means. It can be dangerous for any of the twins because they're mirroring each other. Mirrors show the highest potential that a person can have and the worst version that a person can become. *That* can be scary, so they sometimes choose to separate and be with their soulmates instead."

"And how can you tell if two are twins?"

"Because my husband and I are twins, little missy. The first ones, perhaps. That's why we can be dangerous. Just make sure you aim it towards the opponents and not towards each other, Nika."

"Milady."

Once everyone arrived, we started our supper. It was a relief for me to see Alma getting more relaxed with everyone in the room. She loosened up a little bit, though I could still see her being conscious every now and then. She didn't come from a big family like mine. Our family was an important unit for our lives and for the projects we worked on.

She was a part of it now, so she didn't need to worry that much. I needed to let her know that she was enough. I failed at that once. I knew I had hurt her feelings last night.

23

Reminiscence

Alma

"How is motherhood so far, little missy?" Milady rested her beautiful face on her palm. She looked at me as if it were a staring contest.

"I can't tell yet, Milady. It's only been less than a day." Kolya's hand started rubbing my back. I turned towards him and asked, "How did your mother do it?"

"Haha... I don't know how she did it. We caused her so much trouble. But she was just like that. Nurturing, loving, and feminine with long, fair blonde hair to tangle our fingers with. You know, motherly."

It was funny how everyone suddenly fell into silence. Lance looked as confused as I was. He said, "Why is everyone looking at Kolya like that?"

"We're in shock," Mobhi said.

Adya followed, "Kolya's laughing. That's big news. Keep torturing him, Alma. We like it."

Lance continued, "So, no flip flop to the head from your mother?"

"Eey, that's a Latina and Asian Mami thing." Saint laughed at him.

Frowning, I said, "I don't understand."

"An Asian woman raised Lance. I'm Latino. So we have flip flops in common."

Hristo explained, "Yeah, mother was a Rus, but her family moved around the Balkans when she was little, so..."

"Slippers," the brothers said at almost the same time.

"You know, the leather ones are much heavier than flip flops," Adya added.

"We were her target practise. If father was upset, that was, well..." Seva and Adya finished Klima's sentence, "manageable."

He continued, "But when we upset mother, that was when we were *really* in trouble. Ooo, her eyes changed; only Kolya got the eyes like hers. Father would sit us down as if we were in a courtroom."

"I met Kolya's mother when I lived with them in the forest. She was lovely, by the way. Her cooking, ooh, she could make anything from whatever their fathers caught that day." Joe turned his face towards the brothers, frowning. "How come I've never met the others' mothers?"

"Yes, you have, Joe." Kolman laughed at Joe's recalling face. "Nonna was our mother."

I gasped, covering my mouth. "Your family was in *nevtumgyt?* I thought it was only in the far north and long gone."

"So this youngling truly read history," the Great One said.

Kolya explained, "Ugh, you should see her in the library. If they don't close it, she won't get out."

Saint poured vodka into two glasses. He gave one to Kolya.

"Pour me one, youngling. How do you think we have so many massive archives and libraries if it weren't for my wife?"

Saint gave another glass to the Great One. "Yup, we got a thing for bookworms." They toasted with their glasses.

"Yes, even Lani was a bookworm," Mandy said to me.

"Who was Lani?"

"His fiancée, the one before me."

"And you are okay talking about her?"

"Yeah, yeah, yeah, she might be a sister to our daughter in Heaven. You know, telling the origin story of Papi before *this* Baddie-Daddy version of Max."

"I like the term 'Baddie-Daddy.' It sounds badass," Natasha said, turning her face towards Adya. "Now where's my Baddie-Daddy biker?"

"Practise daddying *here*," Adya answered while showing off Vanya in his arms.

Mia asked, "So you aren't seeing us four as weird?"

The brothers shook their heads. "Why would we be weird?"

"Well, our parents were in exile at the time. Then they freed our two Irish fathers from the pirates," Klima explained. "Kolya's parents were married, Feofan and Nonna. They didn't have any children, even after a long time of marriage. So the wife swapping was necessary for our family."

Hristo followed. "You know, for survival. So his father had an agreement with my father, Krastyo. I was born first, the only Bulgar in the family now."

"After that, an agreement with my father, Roman. He was a Tatar, so we speak a different language from early on. Adya was born first, then me, and then Klima," Seva explained.

Kolman followed, "And then an agreement with my father, Feidhlimidh, after that. Then they had me."

"After that, with my father, Finlugh. Kolman and I were raised with another different language," Mobhi said.

"And then, mother returned to her husband. Finally, Kolya arrived," Hristo added. "So who's marrying whom with you four?"

"The orphan's married to Mia. We need to chain the stray dog. Haha," Sandy answered.

They poured their vodka into the glasses. "To the House of Zhou."

"Oh, I got you, princess. I'll drink it for you." Saint winked at his pregnant wife.

Adya followed, "I got yours, too, Natasha. You can have the light bites." He passed the bread, sausages, luncheon, and cheese to his wife.

For anyone who wasn't familiar with the ritual, they might be thinking about vodka as the party drink. Vodka wasn't to be run down into a digestible drink with sparkling water or soda and lime. Vodka was actually a ritual to celebrate good company or families with light bites in between sips. Conversations and banter were the most suitable companions for vodka.

"You're pregnant, as well?" Mandy looked so excited about the news. "Congratulations."

"To the more, the merrier families."

Here we were, celebrating the newest additions to the family. I never had a big family, but surely I appreciated everyone who welcomed me to their home.

24

Wave

Alma

He put Vanya in his cot after we returned to our suite. He made it clear that we need to train Vanya. As much as I wanted to connect with both the father and son, he convinced me that Vanya needed to understand the difference between me as his Mama and me as Papa's partner. Maybe it was because of the way he was raised, but I followed him for now. There was so much I needed to learn about him.

I prepared the warm water for our bath, although I didn't know if it was warm enough or too hot. "Is it the right temperature?"

He took off his shirt and trousers beside me. "How do you like it?"

"I don't know how I like it. I've never had this before."

He kissed my bare back, and then he touched the water in the bath. "Glad to have your first time. It should be enough." He peeled the rest of my clothes off. Once we were both naked, he got in the bath first.

"Come here, you." When I rested my back on his chest, he poured me with kisses. He started giving me massages on my shoulders. "You like this?"

"Mmm... hmm."

"You are tense, *Dusha Moya*. Relax now. There's nothing to worry about." From my shoulders, his hands moved down to my back as I leaned forward. "I can't read you sometimes. Tell me what's on your mind."

"I'm all right, Kolenka."

He pulled me slowly by the hair and said, "Remember, you're mine. I don't allow you to lie to me." His hands started to claim my breasts. He used my nipples as switches to unlock the truth about me. The truth was that I had been a crab for so long.

My family didn't have much when I was little. Then mum started to work with dad, and I helped to watch my baby sister. Things got better, and my family could afford a nicer house. As the house got bigger, so did the family dynamic.

That was why I had trouble with men with attachment issues. To them, I could easily say, *"It's just a house, not a home. A building of bricks and stones doesn't make it a home."* Or something like, *"It's just a car,"* or *"It's just a thing."*

To Kolya, I couldn't say, "It's just a motorbike" or "It's just a submarine," just as I couldn't say, "It's just a sleigh" to Father Christmas. Firstly, Kolya never owned them. But mainly because he used them for projects and for the right reasons.

Our Great One was right that I became a referee in the family. I was so used to crab-walking from one side to the other between family members. I'd been hard on the outside but mushy on the inside.

Kolya caught this little crab on one of his fishing days. Since then, he had held me captive. He found a way to crack me open. "You better start talking, or I'll make you."

"It's nothing. You don't need to worry about it."

His feet slid under my knees. He locked my legs up wide open. Two digits thrust inside of my pussy while his other hand kept me still by the breast. "You want to keep lying to me? Talk."

"Mmh... Sir." I reached for the back of his neck, hanging onto him. "You said that I'm yours. Hhh... and—umh, your family talked about your parents earlier at supper."

"Keep talking. Your truth is mine." With this kind of pleasure, he made it difficult for me to speak my mind.

"What if I only want to be yours?" Not only were my walls being massaged, but my clit being played by his thumb. "I don't want to be swapped or shared. Hmmh... I, ooh—I want to be only yours, not anybody else's."

"If that's what you want, you better come like my slut should." His cock was growing hard against my back. He squeezed my breasts firmly, both of them in turns. His fingers were praising me generously. "Remember what I told you at your place?"

"No one touches me, not even myself."

"That's right. Look what I did when they took you from me. I took back their entire base. If anyone dares to touch you, I'll bring the burning hell to them. Even the Arctic will melt down and flood."

When he started kissing my neck, he brought me so close to melting down. "Tell me again, what are you?"

"Your slut. Only yours," I said while melting down my release. He caught me so the little crab wouldn't get washed out and get lost in the ocean.

He bent me over to the other side of the bath tub when I was still recovering from my orgasm. This was what I deserved as his captive—to be taken from behind so hard that I couldn't even tell which one was the bath water and which one was sweat.

I was filthy before he caught this crab. The waves from his strokes washed away the dust from my flesh. He held me by the hair, so I could feel each thrust from the power of his ownership. He drowned me in orgasm for the second time. The cum he sprayed purified me from the inside and out. Here was my purification—my initiation to enter his realm. It was the same way that the salt water cleansed and protected a little crab in the ocean.

"Thank you, Sir."

25

Rebuild

Kolya

If anyone spent enough time looking back, the Petrovsky Dock was actually built for building and repairing ships. After we took back the base, we renovated and upgraded it.

We planned to build a pavement runway beside the bush airfield. Vatroslav and other shadow-working aviators were involved in building it. They also planned to build a helipad. Not only the building, but we planned to make it a hub for transport and logistics from sea to air and vice versa. This way, we could complete our projects faster.

Alma decided to reside permanently in Kronshtadt with Vanya. He started to walk, but he hadn't started talking yet. So she taught him signs for his basic needs, hoping that we'd understand what he needed.

She and Mandy also talked frequently, discussing the children. Mandy gave birth to a son in July. They were also on call whenever Natasha needed them with her morning sickness. I liked watching Adya get anxious and even easily panic when it came to Natasha and their unborn baby.

Aside from being a mother, Alma had been working on the archive and its content.
She insisted on preserving the valuables for generations to follow.

Winter was coming in a few weeks. She kept asking to join us to assist our people. I wasn't sure if I could be focused at work with her freezing body. I would be hugging and snuggling her the entire winter instead of working on projects. So I decided to lock her up in one of the fortresses once I returned home.

It was so arousing to see her surrender herself to me. She became my good slut—an even better slut every time I came to see her. She was resting inside one of the cells. Her wrists and ankles were tied for a few good hours.

I woke her up with my fingers combing her hair. "Are you hungry, *Dusha Moya?*"

"Of you, I am, Sir."

"Good." While devouring her lips, I enjoyed the view of her naked body being tied up and held captive. Even with nothing that I had done so far, her nipples were already hard and inviting.

"The girls missed their Daddy. Please, I've missed you, too." Her breasts felt different. They were more sensitive to my touch—softer but fuller. They didn't taste different in my mouth, so it must not be her regime of bodycare.

"*Dusha Moya*, you are different."

"But I don't want to be treated differently." Her lips reached higher to find mine. "I'm still your slut, Sir."

"Of course, I will treat you differently when you are pregnant with my child. I can smell my pup growing inside of you. Why didn't you tell me earlier? I wouldn't tie you like this if I knew." I was about to release her wrists when she rolled her body to hide her wrists under it.

"Because *this* is precisely why. You'd treat me differently." Her tears started falling down her face. "I missed you giving me ropes. You've been gone for two months doing projects."

"There are other ways to remind you that you're mine. And I never like you hiding things from me."

"I—I'm sorry, Sir. I didn't want to distract you at work. You need to catch up before winter comes."

"I told you that I'd taken this womb. It's mine. When you're growing my child in it, I should be the first one to tell. You're not being a good slut by keeping me in the dark. You don't deserve to get these ropes as a reward."

She rolled her body, exposing her tied wrists. She allowed me to untie her wrists and ankles. She kept herself silent, but her tears kept running down her face.

My fingers slipped in between her drenched folds. I gave her a slow and light touch. When I pinched her clit, she writhed and moaned desperately. I kept refusing to give her what she craved the most. "Do you miss me fucking my pussy here?"

She nodded in silence.

"Only a good slut gets used properly, like it's mine."

"But it's your pussy. Please. She missed her owner." Maybe because of the pregnancy hormones, her body reacted differently to me. With each lap of my tongue along her slit and with more friction, the more sweetness her pussy let out.

She wasn't only my slut, but she started to become a beggar for my touch to do the wonderworks on her body. "Please don't stop."

The contrary was precisely what I did to her—stopping when she was so close. "You don't get to ask for anything from me." I pulled her to the edge of the bed to let her head dangle.

"Since when did you know you're pregnant?"

"End of August, about a week after you left for projects."

"Open wide." My cock was out in front of her face. I started to thrust deep into her throat. "If you want to keep a secret..." I hissed. "Make sure it's because my cock's blocking it from getting out."

I denied her once, so it was time for my fingers to start to rebuild her. Her clit was already swollen, and her pussy was desperately drenched. "Did you get morning sickness?" I paused my thrust for her to answer.

She shook her head while still swallowing me. She blinked her tears out with my cock at the back of her throat and my fingers massaging her inner walls. Another finger entered her until I denied her for the second time. She watched me lick my fingers clean.

"Sir, mercy," she whimpered.

"Who else knows?" I lifted her and rested her neck on my arm.

"No one, except the OBGYN. I had an appointment with her to make sure our baby was all right."

I rolled us to the side to spoon her. "What did she say? I could continue fucking you, yes?"

While I was rubbing her womb, she cupped my hand gently. "Of course you can. The doctor said our baby is all right. Please, Sir, have me tonight."

"You should never keep a secret from me. Especially about something important like this one." My cock came home to her from behind.

Inside of her was where I belonged. Her tunnel felt different already. Different good. She felt like she was holding me instead of clenching my cock. Her moans filled the cells to echo.

"I miss my pussy, too." I played with her clit, rebuilding her once again. "Do you think my slut is good enough that I can let you come?"

"Mmm... hmm."

"Come for me. Sink me in your cum." I followed her orgasm with mine. The scent of her hair armoured my naked flesh. In my arms, I showered her with so many kisses. "Be my wife, *Dusha Moya*."

"Hmm, you're late. I feel like I'm already your wife."

One thing never changed; she was my soul to seek refuge in. She sheltered the soul I never thought I had. I didn't think she understood how her wonderworks rebuilt me. My wonderworker was her.

Epilogue
The Evening after Taking Back the Base

"Crown. Prince."

"Speak."

"Put me on the speaker. I know the Wings is there."

"You heard him, youngling. Speak."

"Something that belongs to me is buried in her womb."

Our Great One said, "I continue guarding the North of my origin, even though I'm no longer assigned to it."

"So I heard the Great Prince in Heaven had fallen."

"Fallen I had. Should I bring His Imperial Highness the Great Prince with me?"

To be continued...

Background Stories

Слава Святым.
/Slava Svyatym/
("Glory to the Saints.")

***

This novella was about the House of Svyatoslav, whose name was derived from *Svyat*, which can be translated as "holy," and *Slava*, which could be translated as "glory." Svyatoslav was commonly the first (given) name for a baby boy. Because this publication was so close to her heart, the author decided to use it as a surname in this story. If readers weren't familiar with the Eastern European naming structure, the author hoped that this background story could provide some insights.

N.F. Svyatoslav and A.H. Svyatoslava were mostly addressed only on scholarly or formal occasions. Readers might find other nonfiction publications from the author using the pen name R.L. Zareva for the same reason.

The characters Adya, Seva, and Klima were altered. Historically, patronymic could also function as a surname for a Tatar. For this story, the three Tatar characters and the two Irish characters used the Russified name order. The patronymic of the Tatar characters continued to follow -nov ending pattern.

On less formal occasions, the Slavic people commonly addressed someone by their first name, followed by their patronymic. We addressed the main characters of this book as Nikolai Feofanovich and Alma Hansdotter, in the same way that we addressed the author as Rada Lyubomirova.

Casually, friends and family called the main character Kolya—the general diminutive name—although his brothers might call him Kolyasha. As his partner, Alma called him by the intimate nickname Kolenka.

His fathers referred to him by the baby nickname Nika. Beside 'youngling,' the Great One and Milady also called him Nika. The parents called Ivan Nikolaevich by his baby nickname, Vanka. The grandparents commonly called their grandson Vanyusha. That was the reason the Great One called him that way.

The opponents, Yuren and Yurena, addressed him Kolyan—a slang nickname for undermining their tension of opposition. The author used different diminutives to imply the role of Nikolai Feofanovich and build a holistic storyline in this book.

Saint Nicholas of Myra became the inspiration for the story of Nikolai Feofanovich. He was the Patron Saint of seafarers, unmarried women, prisoners, Russia—particularly Moscow—Greece, and the Swiss city of Fribourg.

With Saint Nicholas of Flüe as the Patron of Switzerland, both Patron Saints gave the author the foundation to build the story in and around Switzerland. Saint Nicholas of Flüe also became the Patron Saint of the Pontifical Swiss Guard.

Among all of the characters in stories that the author has written so far, Kolya was the one with the most layers. There were many legends related to Saint Nicholas that made it feel like home for the author when writing this book.

In this novella, Kolya fulfilled his duties with the call sign "Crown." He was born to parents who practised *nevtumgyt*—partnership by/of wife—for survival in their exile. In the past, it was a practice of the natives who lived in reindeer herding cultures.

The novels *Lord of the Underworld: A Paranormal Shifter Romance of Veles* and

Springtime Birth and Wintertime Rebirth: A Psychic Paranormal Romance of Yarilo and Morana are related to this novella. Veles (or Volos) reemerged in the role of Saint Nicholas after Christianity landed in the Slavic land.

The underworld in ancient Slavic mythology was said to be the land across the sea that flourished and nourished—some might interpret the myth as the southern hemisphere. Veles was believed to be a shifter who turned into a wolf, a bear, or even a dragon and protected the people from Perun's thunder.

The myth of Veles had some similarities with Cernunnos in ancient Celtic mythology. When building an outline of this novella, the author felt the need to include the characters Feidhlimidh and Finlugh. They were to be the remembrance of the Irish who were abducted by pirates and pushed to live away from their origin land.

The author also included the depiction of "The Seven Tiger-Shifters." The legend of the shifters who protected the forest could be read in *The History of Sumatra* by William Marsden (1784).

The character Koloman Mac Feidhlimidh was inspired by the role of Saint Colombanus. He was the Patron Saint of motorcyclists and was said to preserve the Irish tradition. In this story, Kolman operated with the call sign "Celtic" as the navigator for the bikers. Kolman rode a power cruiser because the Patron was believed to love open roads.

Brendan Mac Finlugh, or Mobhi, was inspired by Saint Brendan. The Patron Saint of sailors and travellers was also known as Brendan the Voyager or St. Brendan the Navigator. In this novella, Mobhi used the call sign "Voyage," who became the navigator of Svyat.

Kliment Romanov, whose nickname was Klima, operated with the call sign "Anchor." His character was inspired by Saint Clement, the Patron Saint of seafarers, metalworkers, and stone cutters. It was said that the Patron was drowned by the executor with an anchor tied around his neck.

Hristofor Krastev was inspired by Saint Christopher, the Patron who caressed large families and protected travellers, motorcyclists, drivers, and sailors from bad weather and obstacles. The character Hristo operated on a power cruiser with the call sign "Pilgrim." He was the head of the family, while Kolya was to lead others on projects.

Adrian Romanov and his wife Natasha (a general diminutive of Natalia) were inspired by the story of Saint Adrian. He was the one who patronised guards, soldiers, butchers, and arms dealers. The character Adya was built with a high sense of humour and was a banter starter in the family. The author felt that Adya needed to be the one who led the family to find amusement even in hard times. Riding a sports bike with the call sign "Butcher," Adya was to be a reminder to enjoy every second of life instead of simply killing some time with distractions.

The character Sevastyan Romanov, or Seva, had the call sign "Arrow." Seva was given a sports bike because he was inspired by Saint Sebastian, the Patron of athletes and archers.

The author hoped that the readers would enjoy reading this book as much as the author enjoyed writing it. Whether you were a motorcyclist, driver, seafarer, or aviator, make it home. If you were a traveller away from your origins, may every step you took be sheltered and protected under the Patrons' care.

About the Author

Rada Lyubomirova retells the myths, legends, and folktales with a darker taste and morally grey characters. Each story is to reimagine childhood stories in either historical or contemporary literary art. Her works are to give rebirth to the timeless narratives that have enthralled generations.

Her writing style is a tasteful blend of dark romance with a medium-to-fast burn rate. Classic stories are given a seductively darker twist to guide you with a passion that will keep you delightfully hooked deep into the night.

As the author enjoys her travel time, her books invite you to take an enchanting journey through exotic lands to return to treasured childhood memories. By meeting people from different cultural backgrounds, the author finds that myths, legends, and folktales may unite people.

Through exploring foreign lands, the author sees the commonalities that connect cultures through stories. She finds it fascinating how these tales travel across borders and unite people in a sense of wonder and value to pass down to the next generation.

Rada cherishes the bond and collaboration she has with her readers. Your feedback shapes and enhances the realms she creates in the literary arts. Is there another tale, legend, or folktale that has fascinated you? Leave your thoughts and reviews on her stories.

About the Publisher

Besides publishing fiction and non-fiction books, Compendia Publishing creates content for social media and online courses.

Scan the QR code above to see our portfolio of work.

***

162

Thank you for purchasing the original copy of this book.
Your feedback will help both the author and the publisher with future works.